▶▶▶ACCEL·WORLD

ARCHANGEL OF SAVAGE LIGHT

REKI
KAWAHARA
ILLUSTRATION BY
HIMA
DESIGN BY
bee-pee

AQUA CURRENT/AKIRA AND ASH RO

Cyan Pile
TAKUMU

Silver Crow
HARUYUKI

Lime Bell
CHIYURI

Blood Leopard
PARD

LLER/RIN RESCUE MISSION, START!

Black Lotus
KUROYUKIHIME

Sky Raker
FUKO

Ardor Maiden
UTAI

Scarlet Rain
NIKO

"—Our wound shall be healed with your lamentations. —Sacrifice your many glories to us."

"..."

"Shake it off...!"

SEIRYU

Super-class Enemy guarding the Castle's east gate. One of the Four Gods.

METATRON

Legend-class Enemy.
An archangel guarding the
headquarters of the Acceleration
Research Society.

ACCELERATED WORLD LEGION DISTRIBUTION MAP

ITABASHI WARD

KITA WARD

ADACHI WARD
YELLOW LEGION,
CRYPT COSMIC CIRCUS

KATSUSHIKA
WARD

NERIMA WARD
RED LEGION,
PROMINENCE

PATISSERIE
LA PLAGE

TOSHIMA
WARD

SUNSHINE CITY

ARAKAWA WARD

SUMIDA
WARD

NAKANO
WARD

BUNKYO WARD
BLUE LEGION, LEONIDS

TAITO
WARD

SUGINAMI WARD

SHINJUKU WARD

TOKYO SKYTREE

BLACK LEGION,
NEGA NEBULUS

KOENJI STATION

AKIHABARA

CHIYODA WARD

EDOGAWA WARD

UMESATO JUNIOR
HIGH SCHOOL

GOVERNMENT
BUILDING

IMPERIAL PALACE

MATSUNOGI ACADEMY
ELEMENTARY DIVISION

KOTO
WARD

SASAZUKA GIRLS' ACADEMY
MIDDLE SCHOOL DIVISION

SHIBUYA
WARD

TOKYO MIDTOWN
TOWER

CHUO WARD

PURPLE LEGION, AURORA OVAL

GREEN LEGION,
GREAT WALL

MINATO
WARD

OLD TOKYO TOWER

SETAGAYA
WARD

WHITE LEGION,
OSCILLATORY UNIVERSE

MEGURO
WARD

SHINAGAWA
WARD

OTA WARD

ACCELERATED WORLD

Imperial Palace

This building sits in a location corresponding with the Imperial Palace in the real world. Gates rise up in the east, west, north, and south of the Castle, and each is guarded by one of four Super-class Enemies, the strongest of the strong. These Enemies—the Four Gods—have an absolute status, boasting a strength far greater than that of Legend-class ones. They are Genbu of the north, Suzaku of the south, Byakko of the west, and Seiryu of the east gate.

At the south gate with Suzaku, Ardor Maiden was once held prisoner due to an Unlimited Enemy Kill. Graphite Edge is apparently also being held at the north gate with Genbu. Currently, Nega Nebulus is setting out to rescue Aqua Current, who is imprisoned at Seiryu's east gate.

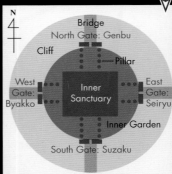

N

Bridge
North Gate: Genbu

Cliff

Pillar

West
Gate:
Byakko

Inner
Sanctuary

East
Gate:
Seiryu

Inner Garden

South Gate: Suzaku

▶▶▶ *ACCEL • WORLD* 14

ARCHANGEL OF SAVAGE LIGHT

Reki Kawahara

Illustrations: HIMA

Design: bee-pee

NEW YORK

■ Kuroyukihime = Umesato Junior High School student council vice president. Trim and clever girl who has it all. Her background is shrouded in mystery. Her in-school avatar is a spangle butterfly she programmed herself. Her duel avatar is the Black King, Black Lotus (level nine).

■ Haruyuki = Haruyuki Arita. Eighth grader at Umesato Junior High School. Bullied, on the pudgy side. He's good at games, but shy. His in-school avatar is a pink pig. His duel avatar is Silver Crow (level five).

■ Chiyuri = Chiyuri Kurashima. Haruyuki's childhood friend. Meddling, energetic girl. Her in-school avatar is a silver cat. Her duel avatar is Lime Bell (level four).

■ Takumu = Takumu Mayuzumi. A boy Haruyuki and Chiyuri have known since childhood. Good at kendo. His duel avatar is Cyan Pile (level five).

■ Fuko = Fuko Kurasaki. Burst Linker belonging to the old Nega Nebulus. One of the Four Elements. Lived as a recluse due to certain circumstances but was persuaded by Kuroyukihime and Haruyuki to come back to the battlefront. Taught Haruyuki about the Incarnate System. Her duel avatar is Sky Raker (level eight).

■ Uiui = Utai Shinomiya. Burst Linker belonging to the old Nega Nebulus. One of the Four Elements. Fourth grader in the elementary division of Matsunogi Academy. Not only can she use the advanced curse removal command "Purify," she is also skilled at long-range attacks. Her duel avatar is Ardor Maiden (level seven).

■ Current = Formally known as Aqua Current. Real name: Akira Himi. Burst Linker belonging to the old Nega Nebulus. One of the Four Elements. Rules water. Known as "The One," the bouncer who undertakes the protection of new Burst Linkers.

■ Graphite Edge = Real name: unknown. Burst Linker belonging to the old Nega Nebulus. One of the Four Elements. Their identity is still wrapped in mystery.

■ Neurolinker = A portable Internet terminal that connects with the brain via a wireless quantum connection and enhances all five senses with images, sounds, and other stimuli.

■ Brain Burst = Neurolinker application sent to Haruyuki by Kuroyukihime.

■ Duel avatar = Player's virtual self, operated when fighting in Brain Burst.

■ Legion = Groups composed of many duel avatars with the objective of expanding occupied areas and securing rights. There are seven main Legions, each led by one of the Seven Kings of Pure Color.

■ Normal Duel Field = The field where normal Brain Burst battles (one-on-one) are carried out. Although the specs do possess elements of reality, the system is essentially on the level of an old-school fighting game.

■ Unlimited Neutral Field = Field for high-level players where only duel avatars at levels four and up are allowed. The game system is of a wholly different order than that of the Normal Duel Field, and the level of freedom in this field beats out even the next-generation VRMMO.

■ Movement Control System = System in charge of avatar control. Normally, this system handles all avatar movement.

■ Image Control System = System in which the player creates a strong image in their mind to operate the avatar. The mechanism is very different from the normal Movement Control System, and very few players can use it. Key component of the Incarnate System.

■ Incarnate System = Technique allowing players to interfere with the Brain Burst program's Image Control System to bring about a reality outside of the game's framework. Also referred to as "overwriting" game phenomena.

■ Acceleration Research Society = Mysterious Burst Linker group. They do not think of Brain Burst as a simple fighting game and are planning something. Black Vise and Rust Jigsaw are members.

■ Armor of Catastrophe = An Enhanced Armament also called "Chrome Disaster." Equipped with this, an avatar can use powerful abilities such as Drain, which absorbs the HP of the enemy avatar, and Divination, which calculates enemy attacks in advance to evade them. However, the spirit of the wearer is polluted by Chrome Disaster, which comes to rule the wearer completely.

■ Star Caster = The longsword carried by Chrome Disaster. Although it now has a sinister form, it was originally a famous and solemn sword that shone like a star, just as the name suggests.

■ ISS kit = Abbreviation for "IS mode study kit." ("IS mode" is "Incarnate System mode.") The kit allows any duel avatar who uses it to make use of the Incarnate System. While using it, a red "eye" is attached to some part of the avatar, and a black aura overlay—the staple of Incarnate attacks— is emitted from the eye.

■ Seven Arcs = The seven strongest Enhanced Armaments in the Accelerated World. They are the greatsword Impulse, the staff Tempest, the large shield Strife, the Luminary (form unknown), the straight sword Infinity, the full-body armor Destiny, and the Fluctuating Light (form unknown).

■ Mental-Scar Shell = The emotional scars that are the foundation of a duel avatar (mental scars created from trauma in early childhood)—this is the shell enveloping them. Children with exceptionally hard and thick "shells" are said to produce metal-color duel avatars.

■ Artificial metal color = Refers to a metal-color avatar that is not generated naturally from the subject's mental scars, but rather produced artificially by a third party through the thickening of the Mental-Scar Shell.

■ Unlimited EK = Abbreviation for Unlimited Enemy Kill. The subject avatar is killed by a powerful Enemy in the Unlimited Neutral Field, and each time they regenerate (after a fixed period of time), they are killed again by that Enemy, falling into an infinite hell.

▶▶▶ *ACCEL·WORLD*

1

"Do you remember, C?"

Haruyuki shifted his gaze at the sudden question and found that, at some point, a small figure had come to stand next to him.

The armor of her upper body, patterned after a white Japanese robe, was the color of unbleached fabric, the whitest shade available, with pure, natural-fiber materials. Meanwhile, the *hakama* she wore on her lower half was a brilliant red, a fresh yet solemn color, while her avatar's long hair hung down to the belt around her waist, covering her slender back. She exuded the overall impression of an ethereal shrine maiden.

One of the Four Elements who formed the senior executive council within the Black Legion, Nega Nebulus, and also known by the name Testarossa, Ardor Maiden looked up at Haruyuki with her cool, cherubic eye lenses. "...Do you remember what you said to me a little over ten days ago, when we were locked up inside the Castle?"

"Uh, um..." Unable to immediately answer Maiden's—aka Utai Shinomiya's—question, Haruyuki scratched the metallic helmet of his own duel avatar, Silver Crow, with the tips of his fingers.

Naturally, he clearly remembered from beginning to end how

they had charged into the only area in the Accelerated World where entry was prohibited, which corresponded to the Imperial Palace in the real world—the Castle. Groups of super-powerful soldier Enemies patrolled the inside, and if they hadn't been able to find a way out, Utai and Haruyuki would have no doubt ended up in a kind of pseudo–Unlimited EK situation.

Their exploration of the Castle had taken a full night, including breaks, and during that time, they had talked about any number of things. Thus, now, ten days later, the mental acuity he needed to pinpoint exactly which conversation Utai was talking about was—

Suddenly, the plate under his feet shuddered fiercely, and Haruyuki opened his wings slightly to keep his balance. As he did, he reached out to support Maiden's back with his left hand; the female avatar neatly dipped her head in thanks.

"Sorry!" A voice came through a speaker up ahead. *"There was, like, this huge hole in the road! Anyone fall off?!"*

"NP." The reply came from an avatar opposite Haruyuki and Utai, who sported a deep-crimson leopard head: Blood Leopard. The other passengers—the Black King, Black Lotus; her deputy Sky Raker; Cyan Pile; and Lime Bell—also snapped to attention and stared out ahead of the vehicle as it roared forward.

Haruyuki and the other members of Nega Nebulus, together with Pard, the Submaster of the Red Legion, Prominence—a total of seven people—were careening down the Century End stage road on a massive, twelve-wheeled armored trailer. Sitting in the cockpit was none other than the master of Prominence, the Red King, Scarlet Rain.

The treacherous vehicle held four auto cannons on the front of the tractor, multiple missile pods on the trailer area (which was where Haruyuki and the others were standing), and had large-diameter laser guns equipped on both sides. Not to mention that the trailer itself was the Enhanced Armament "Invincible," transformed into a sort of souped-up tank by the Red

King—who also boasted the nickname Immobile Fortress in the Accelerated World.

At Niko's voice command, the trailer—Dreadnought—had departed from Umesato Junior High in Suginami about five minutes earlier and was currently barreling down a back street in Nakano Area No. 2. The shortest route to their objective, the Castle's east gate, was to go straight down Oume Highway eastward, turn onto Shinjuku Street after passing the Yamanote Line, and then get onto Uchibori Street via Gyoen Mae and Yotsuya, but the major roads in the Unlimited Neutral Field were patrolled by Beast-class Enemies.

Naturally, with a battle formation that included two kings, they could easily dispatch even a Beast class without really breaking a sweat. But a large part of their route was also in territory controlled by the Blue Legion, Leonids. If a Leonids Enemy-hunting party happened upon them, they were highly unlikely to let the Nega Nebulus team pass through with a wink and a smile.

Given all this, the massive trailer was deliberating staying off the wide Oume Highway, but the Century End stage roads were peppered with sinkholes and overturned oil drums and other obstacles. They were not good roads by any standard. And there was no space to avoid obstacles on these back streets, so they shook rather spectacularly. But not once did they become stuck or collide with a building as they went; Niko's skill was to be commended.

Standing alongside Utai at the very end of the trailer, Haruyuki considered this as he looked up at the sky of the Unlimited Neutral Field. Dense black clouds loomed overhead, but he spotted the light of the stars from time to time through faint breaks. Because the star map of the Accelerated World re-created the real world's constellations, given that it was June, the large Summer Triangle would be hanging low in the eastern sky.

Haruyuki had learned about it during the time he had been locked up in the Castle with Utai. While they'd sat there, trapped,

Utai had indicated a star with her small hand—Altair—and then had related that the initial Burst Linkers had also looked up at the starry night sky, and that was why the names of the major Legions were all related to space.

Nega Nebulus was a dark nebula. Prominence was a flare on the sun. The Leonids were an annual meteor shower.

According to independent research on Haruyuki's part once they'd managed to make it safely out of the Castle, the name of the Green Legion, Great Wall, referred to a wall formed by a collection of countless galaxies in a place two hundred million light-years away from Earth. Similarly, the Purple Legion, Aurora Oval, indicated an elliptical area enclosing the poles of the Earth where auroras frequently occurred. The Yellow Legion, Crypt Cosmic Circus, seemed to be the only Legion whose name had no relation to space terminology, the sort of move you'd expect from a contrarian like Yellow Radio. And the White Legion, Oscillatory Universe, clearly indicated the scientific concept of an oscillating universe.

This one was the hardest for Haruyuki to wrap his mind around. The oscillating universe theory was initially espoused nearly a hundred years earlier, and put simply, it stated that the universe repeatedly expanded and collapsed. The expansion was the Big Bang, which even Haruyuki had heard more than a little about, while the collapse was called the Big Crunch. The universe, over however many billions of years, cycled through Big Bangs and Big Crunches—creation and destruction—and at some point, the current universe, including Earth and the Milky Way, would contract into a single tiny dot. Or that was the main idea, but this oscillating universe theory had apparently been refuted and shelved long ago.

So then, why had the White King, White Cosmos—also known as Transient Eternity—apparently deliberately named her Legion after a discarded theory?

Naturally, Haruyuki's knowledge did not extend this far. The little sister of the White King in the real, Kuroyukihime, perhaps might have known, but he definitely couldn't just ask her about it. The White King was the very person who had cleverly manipulated Kuroyukihime into sending the Red King, Red Rider, into total point loss; and the reason Kuroyukihime currently lived alone in a town house in Asagaya Jutaku was a family incident brought about by her intensifying anger and hatred toward her sister.

It had already been three days since Kuroyukihime explained all this to him. She'd told him the story in a pained voice, with a grief-stricken look, when they were alone in the student council office after school. The lurid tale started with the Seven Kings of Pure Color reaching level nine and continued up to the eventual destruction of the initial Nega Nebulus.

When, two days earlier, on Friday, she and Fuko Kurasaki had stayed over at Haruyuki's house, Kuroyukihime had looked like she was back to her old self. He hadn't sensed anything especially different about her in the Territories the day before or at the school festival that day, either.

But there was no way that could be. He knew there were still ripples disturbing the calm of her heart. Because the reason she had become so upset to begin with—the mystery of Red Rider's crest, etched into the sealed ISS kit cards Haruyuki had obtained in the Setagaya area—still hadn't been resolved.

He brought his gaze back down from the night sky and stared at the slender back of the Black King as she stood in the center of the trailer. While everyone else shuddered and shook with the vehicle, Kuroyukihime alone, with her hovering ability, maintained an essentially static position. Arms crossed, legs neatly lined up, she was almost like a single black sword. Seeing her from behind like this, Haruyuki couldn't help but feel the strength and brittleness of her sharply honed blades.

Of the eight there, it was likely Kuroyukihime who had the greatest, most serious expectations. Their first objective: rescue Aqua Current, trapped in Unlimited EK at the east gate of the Castle. Their second: the destruction of the ISS kit main body, hidden away in Tokyo's Midtown Tower. Both objectives were directly connected to the events that had occurred two years and ten months earlier.

They had already been reunited with Current in the real world, and they had taken pains to learn everything they could from her about her situation, so that the first mission simply required the resolve to go and do it. But there was still a large unknown at play in the second mission: the relationship between the ISS kits and the first Red King, Red Rider. As long as the mystery of the crossed-guns crest remained unsolved, they couldn't know what would happen at Midtown Tower. They might be thrust up against some obstacle other than the Legend-class Enemy Archangel Metatron that guarded the tower.

But.

Haruyuki clenched his right hand into a tight fist and vowed in his heart: *No matter what happens, I will protect Kuroyukihime. And not just her—Taku, Chiyu, Master Fuko, Shinomiya, Curren, Pard, and Niko, too, I'll protect them all. I mean, they're all helping me save Rin and Ash, without even complaining. We're totally going to smash the ISS kit main body and go back to the real world together. And then I'm going to properly introduce Rin and Pard and Niko to Curren and Shinomiya, and we'll get back to the school festival—*

"Oh..."

Here, Haruyuki finally stumbled upon the crux of Utai's question. He turned his gaze back toward Ardor Maiden, who was still standing next to him, and the small shrine maiden avatar seemed to read Haruyuki's mind.

"Have you remembered then, C?" she said as if grinning.

"Y-yeah. I told you in the Castle, right? That I had a friend I wanted to introduce you to."

"That's exactly right." Utai nodded sharply and turned her eyes to the front, toward the cockpit they couldn't see from the back of the trailer. "The friend you spoke of at that time was the Red King, Scarlet Rain, wasn't it?"

"Yeah." Returning her nod, he traveled back in his memory twelve days.

Haruyuki had indeed said that to Utai after they'd managed to slip into the main building of the Castle, when they were walking along the wooden floor of the central hallway: that once they managed to escape from the Castle and solve all the various problems before them, he had a friend he wanted to introduce her to. *"Kinda sassy, kinda rough, but...but she's really great. Maybe you could be friends with her, too."*

Yet, he hadn't been able to finish the sentence at the time. He'd been suddenly overcome by a terrible premonition that it would never happen, that some catastrophe would befall them before he could introduce Utai to Niko. But in the end, this premonition turned out to be needless fretting on his part.

On the twenty-fourth day of this month, four days after their escape from the Castle, Niko and Utai had met at the curry party held at the Arita house and spoken, albeit briefly. The main purpose of that gathering had been a training session to help Haruyuki acquire the Theoretical Mirror ability, so they had hurriedly moved to the Unlimited Neutral Field. But they could try again, once the current mission was over. He would show Niko, Pard, and Rin to the animal hutch in the rear courtyard and reintroduce them to Utai and to Hoo.

Haruyuki made this promise in his heart and then said to Utai, "...But now that I'm thinking about it, I didn't actually have to bring you guys together. You and Niko—er, Rain—met each other ages ago, Mei. In the territories between Negabu and Promi, way back when."

"Yes. But we only were able to say hello once on the battlefield, and of course, we had never met in the real. I'm truly delighted that you introduced Rain to me, C...We're both red colors; I'm sure we'll be able to be friends."

"Yeah. I know you will...I just know it," he replied, half for his own benefit, before bringing his face back up.

Toward the front of the trailer that was roaring down the road, a remarkably massive building appeared on the right, in the midst of half-destroyed buildings. The distinctive silhouette of the twin towers was, without a doubt, that of the Diet, Tokyo's main government building. The tip of the five-hundred-meter-tall edifice was completely cloaked in twisting black clouds.

Rumor had it that the throne of the Blue King, Blue Knight, sat on the special viewing platform at the top of that building in the Unlimited Neutral Field. Naturally, the king himself wasn't always seated there, but there was a 0.0001 percent chance that the level-niner Niko, called an Originator, was glaring down at the world below from the summit that Haruyuki was currently staring up at.

According to the original schedule, the mission to invade Midtown Tower was to have taken place the following weekend after the fourth meeting of the Seven Kings, to be held in a few days. The attack party was to have been made up of elites carefully selected from all the Legions, with perhaps even Blue Knight and Green Grandé participating, which would give the attack force fighting power on a scale far and away beyond that which the eight on the trailer at that moment could manage (well, the nine of them, if you counted Aqua Current's eventual participation).

But just as Kuroyukihime had said before they sallied, there was a possibility that information from the meetings of the Seven Kings was being funneled to the Acceleration Research Society through the Quad Eyes Analyst, Argon Array. So naturally, the Acceleration Research Society was likely to be waiting to greet the attack party with a multitude of clever traps that played to their specialty. So a plan where a large party basically marched on the front door didn't seem to be the best strategy.

Put another way, to succeed in the surprise assault strategy that the nine had adopted that day, they would have to attack with the perfect combination of shock and speed. They had to render Metatron helpless, swiftly penetrate Midtown Tower, and destroy the ISS kit main body before the Acceleration Research Society noticed them.

A critical component of this strategy was the Optical Conduction ability Haruyuki had acquired, and whether or not this power—a counterfeit of the Theoretical Mirror he had originally been trying to get—would work against Metatron's instant-death laser. This was directly connected to the success or failure of the overall mission; he probably should have taken a shot from Invincible's main armament before the big day just to make sure this ability would actually reflect it.

But it wasn't as though they had the time for him to train and try for the mirror ability again if he did fail. And even if he did deflect Niko's lasers, that wasn't proof he could do the same thing with Metatron's. With things where they were now, Haruyuki was better off believing, rather than doubting. .

In himself. And in Chiyuri and Utai and his precious friends who had given everything they had to helping him obtain his current abilities.

The trailer passed the northern side of the Diet and pulled onto Yasukuni Street from a back road. Soon enough, he could see the large guardrails on the north side of Shinjuku Station. The massive armored vehicle made the earth shake as it approached the underpass to slip below the overhead bridge of the Yamanote train line.

"...Ah, crap." Niko's voice came suddenly from the speaker.

"State the nature of your 'crap,' Red King," Kuroyukihime immediately replied.

"Nah, I was just thinking it's gonna be a tight squeeze here. And by tight, I mean for you guys up on top."

"..."

They all fell silent and stared doubtfully at the guardrails rapidly drawing near. Indeed, given the distance from the road to the bridge, it seemed the vehicle would clear it somehow, just barely, but any way they looked at it, the heads of the seven passengers on the roof would slam into the steel frame—and that likely wouldn't be the only hit they took.

"C-come on! Now that you've realized that, you can just stop, can't you?!" Kuroyukihime's voice was strained now that she understood the situation, but the vehicle's twelve spinning wheels showed no signs of slackening.

"Nah, the thing about that, see, this thing doesn't have any brakes." Niko's reply was nonchalant over the roar of the trailer's engine.

"Wh…wh…what?!"

"So, like, Lotus, I'mma let you handle this. Over an' out."

"Not 'over and out'! A car without any brakes, I mean, that's like…Aaah…" Apparently, Kuroyukihime couldn't immediately come up with a suitable analogy.

Beside her, Fuko casually remarked from her wheelchair, "They say love is like a car without brakes, but the opposite metaphor is difficult, hmm?"

"…How can you be so utterly relaxed, Raker?"

"Oh my, when push comes to shove, I *do* have Gale Thruster, after all."

"Th-that's not really fair!"

Haruyuki's heart raced as he listened to this conversation between Legion Master and Submaster, and he realized, *Oh, I can fly. So NP.* But he really shouldn't escape into the sky on his own.

The trailer started down the hill directly in front of the steel bridge, picking up even more speed.

Then came a firm voice: "Please leave it to me, Master!"

Cyan Pile—Takumu—his body wrapped in heavy indigo-blue armor, took a few steps forward. He readied the Enhanced Armament of his right arm, Pile Driver, as he shouted, "I figured something like this might happen, so I made sure to fully charge my special-attack gauge! Here we go! Lightning Cyan Spike!!"

The steel spike poking out of the barrel of the Enhanced Armament became a pale-blue lance of light and shot forward in a straight line. The superheated plasma instantly ripped through the rust-covered steel of the overhead bridge, gouging out a hole about ten centimeters wide before disappearing into the eastern Shinjuku sky.

And that was it. The bridge continued to exist in front of them, not destroyed nor flying through the air. Lightning Cyan Spike, a level-four special attack, was a powerful technique with both piercing and heat characteristics, but because the force was concentrated in one spot, when it struck a sparse object, the majority of the energy plunged out to the rear, which made it not so useful for large-scale destruction.

Or so Haruyuki suspected.

As he built his mental hypothesis, his friend Takumu stood rooted to the spot, astonished, and Chiyuri patted his arm consolingly.

A few seconds later, Kuroyukihime nodded deeply. "No, well, we mustn't waste Pile's efforts," she intoned solemnly. "Leave the rest to me." Arms still crossed, she moved to the very front of the trailer, switched places with Pard encamped there, and smoothly raised the sword of her right leg. The distance to the bridge was a mere five—three—meters...

"Death by Barraging."

At the same time as she voiced the technique name, the Black King's right leg transformed into a conical shadow. It hadn't lost its physical substance; it was just kicking outward repeatedly at incredible speed. Even Haruyuki's eyes couldn't completely capture the multiple blows—reaching a hundred hits in an instant.

The trailer cockpit charged into the overhead bridge, the edges scraping along the metal, sending sparks flying. On the verge of smashing into Kuroyukihime, the girder broke up into innumerable metallic fragments that shot off to both sides. Black Lotus's leg dug farther into the steel bridge, opening up the hole Cyan Pile had gouged out. Haruyuki expected it to be noisier, with more sparks; it was like she was cutting through craft paper rather than metal.

With the Black King transformed into a boring machine, Pard crouched down behind her, and so the others also hurried to their knees all in a line (Fuko stayed in her wheelchair). In less than three seconds, the tank had passed through and come out onto the east side of the Yamanote Line.

In the rear, Haruyuki looked back to see that a large hole, around a meter and a half wide, had been gouged out of the steel bridge.

"'Ro's footwork is as frightening as ever," Utai noted coolly from her place crouched down in front of him.

"And her handiwork's plenty scary, too," Haruyuki added quietly.

Kuroyukihime brought her right leg down smoothly and headed back to the center of the vehicle roof.

"Mmm," she directed at a slightly glum-looking Takumu after clearing her throat. "...Pile, don't get so down. I was the one who told you to extend your powers in line with your avatar characteristics, after all. I know there'll be a situation when you save us all with your technique's piercing ability."

"Y...yes, I understand that. But lately, I've been thinking it might be a good idea to expand the breadth of my attack abilities a little..."

"A difficult problem," Fuko added gently. She moved her wheelchair forward a little and continued from Kuroyukihime's side. "Which should you aim for: all-rounder or specialist? This is a topic that has been debated since the earliest days of the Accelerated World, and in the more than seven years that have passed since then, no one has come up with an answer. Or I suppose, to be more precise, I should say the answer is different for each Legion. Our policy in Nega Nebulus is 'If you can't decide, specialize!' but there are many all-purpose avatars in Aurora Oval and CCC. And Prominence's policy is?"

"*Specialize and specialize some more, o'course!*"

All present nodded at Niko's excited voice coming through the speaker. The Red King, Scarlet Rain, was basically a classic example of an avatar hyper-specialized in long-distance firepower. Her deputy Blood Leopard, seated at the front of the trailer, was also specialized in agility and biting attacks, even though she was a red type.

"Ooh! I've got a question!" Now it was Chiyuri raising her

hand. "But, like, if you get too specialized, don't you have zero hope of winning sometimes when you get dragged into a stage you're not compatible with? I mean, an extreme example would be, like, an avatar specialized in fire attacks not being able to do anything in an Ocean stage since all the fighting's in the water. So I was just kinda wondering about that, too, you know?"

"Normally, that would be exactly right." Smiling, Fuko readily agreed with Chiyuri. She turned her eyes toward Utai, standing next to Haruyuki. "For instance, Ardor Maiden is the duel avatar in Nega Nebulus most specialized in long-distance firepower. But it can hardly be said that she is compatible with a water-type stage, because her main weapon, the flame arrow, disappears in a heavy rain, much less in the middle of an ocean. Maiden must have also hit a wall of her own around level four or five. Isn't that right, Mei?"

Utai bobbed her head up and down. Perhaps because of the attention suddenly focused on her, she shrank into herself, embarrassed.

"...But Maiden didn't seek out some power of a different affinity." Warm eyes still fixed upon the small shrine maiden, the sky-blue avatar told the story: "She instead intently refined her own abilities. And then her duel avatar responded to that intent. Mei, the most powerful flames you can produce now—with a normal special attack, of course—how far can they penetrate in the sea of an Ocean stage?"

"Um...probably around thirty meters, I guess," Utai responded bashfully, and the three junior members of the group—Haruyuki, Takumu, and Chiyuri—opened their eyes wide in surprise.

"...Maiden," Takumu said after a minute or two, incredulous. "So then a fire attack you launch in the water will travel thirty meters without disappearing?"

Utai only bobbed her head silently, so Kuroyukihime spoke on her behalf:

"I remember it being about half that range, when I saw it way back when. So you've kept working on it since then, Maiden?

Those flames charging through the ocean, churning the water into a white foam, that was really beautiful."

"Wow! I want to see it, too!" Chiyuri cried out in delight. "Maybe the next Change will be an Ocean stage!"

"Whoa!" Niko shouted roughly from the cockpit. *"Careful what you wish for there! My tank'll sink to the bottom!"*

"NP. Just develop a battleship mode," Pard retorted, and everyone burst into bright laughter.

"I understand, Master. Raker." Takumu nodded deeply once the giggles had subsided. "In short, it's a matter of how much faith you have in your duel avatar. My mind produced Cyan Pile here, and no matter what happens, I'm going to believe in this guy...Though I also have an important promise to keep with Haru."

Takumu turned to Silver Crow at this last note, and Haruyuki heard his intent loud and clear.

Five days earlier in Takumu's room, when Haruyuki had gone over after his first battle with Wolfram Cerberus had left him utterly trounced, the two best friends had made a promise. That once they reached level seven—the entrance to being known as *high rankers*—then the two would face off for real, with everything they had. This was still a long way off, given that neither had even made it to level six, but they could never forget this vow even for a moment. Because all their fights, all their experience in the Accelerated World, led directly to that time that would someday come.

"That's right, Taku," Haruyuki said, forcefully taking a step forward now. "And I mean, Silver Crow is specialized on the one point of flight ability, so I'm not thinking of trying to make him all-purpose at this stage of the game. Our duel avatars aren't game characters given to us by the system..."

"...They're avatars of our own selves."

The two boys nodded meaningfully at each other.

"...What's this about?" Chiyuri looked slightly creeped out. "You guys got some big-deal promise?"

"Um, sorry, Chii, this is—"

"A promise between two men isn't something you go 'round telling everyone!" Haruyuki cried, thrusting his chest forward.

The third member of the group of childhood friends glared at him. "I feel like when you guys keep secrets, it generally develops into a whole thing, though," she commented doubtfully.

"Th-that's not true! I mean, up to now, the only things that have been a big deal are, um..."

*That and that. Oh, that. That, too...*Watching Haruyuki count off with the fingers of his right hand, the girls all shook their heads in exasperation as one.

While this conversation was going on, the armored truck continued to race ahead full speed, passing by the northern side of Shinjuku Gyoen and drawing near Yotsuya Station. If they drove a few minutes more, they would plunge into Hanzomon in the real world—the western gate of the Castle in the Accelerated World.

Kuroyukihime and Fuko had led a team from the former Nega Nebulus to challenge the Super-class Enemy guarding that gate—Byakko, one of the Four Gods. Although they had been trampled by the claws and tusks of the divine beast, which boasted a terrible and powerful speed, they managed to just barely escape Byakko's territory, thanks to Fuko's Gale Thruster. So now, the west gate was the only one of the Castle's four gates that had no one sealed away at it. Thus, for the time being at least, Haruyuki wouldn't get the chance to see the beast. Not until Nega Nebulus once again took on the challenge of a Castle attack.

The trailer passed Yotsuya Station and climbed up a gentle slope to reveal an enormous silhouette up ahead. Given that this was the Century End stage, all buildings should have been half-destroyed, but there was not a single blemish on the high Castle walls; they rose darkly up into the sky. The design of the main building, faintly visible on the other side of the walls, brought together ancient Gothic keynotes with modern hardness. The flickering of countless watch fires in the night fog was eerily beautiful.

The Castle in the Unlimited Neutral Field, unlike the palace in the real world, carved out a perfect circle 1.5 kilometers in diameter. It was surrounded by a bottomless ravine, above which an abnormally powerful gravity was at work, meaning that neither Haruyuki's wings nor Fuko's booster could make it across. The only means of getting to the other side of the ravine were the thirty-meter-wide bridges connecting the Castle to the gates at the cardinal points.

Niko brought the truck/tank out onto Shinjuku Street from the back road and cut power momentarily at the T-intersection where it hit Uchibori Street, so that they naturally decelerated. Ahead of them, the great bridge—and the gate—were visible, but the God Byakko would open its eyes only if they stepped onto it. All twelve wheels screeched as the trailer turned sharply right, onto the road stretching out along the infinite cliff, before the engine roared back to life, and they began to race to the south.

Haruyuki went over to the left side of the vehicle and looked up at the dark wall rising up into the sky beyond the five hundred meters of ravine. On the other side of that wall lived countless sentinel Enemies and one boy Burst Linker. Of course, he wasn't always in a dive, but he had talked like he spent a lot of time on this side, so the probability that he was right then, at that moment, a mere thousand meters away, was probably higher than that of the Blue King being at the government building.

At the time of the Castle escape mission ten days earlier, Haruyuki had promised that they would meet again someday—he and the young samurai avatar who held the Arc of Infinity, Trilead Tetroxide. In the mission to rescue Aqua Current that was about to start, they weren't planning to charge all the way into the Castle, although that had also been the case during the previous mission to rescue Ardor Maiden. Still, Haruyuki couldn't help hoping that he and his young friend would be reunited that day.

But we'll definitely meet again one day, Lead, Haruyuki resolved, as if calling out silently to the other side of the wall.

Utai smiled and nodded, almost as though she could hear his thoughts.

The tank continued to charge along the curving Uchibori Street until it finally passed in front of the south gate, which was guarded by the God Suzaku.

The place where Ardor Maiden had been locked away until ten days earlier...Haruyuki looked out onto the wasteland to the right, which was likely Hibiya Park in the real world, as their trajectory gradually shifted to the north.

Right around the time the office buildings in the Marunouchi neighborhood started to appear from the within the darkness, the vehicle's speed dropped. They coasted along another hundred meters or so on inertia before the tank came to a halt in the middle of a large intersection.

"Last stop! Castle, east gate! All passengers, pleeeaaase disembark! ♪"

Obeying the announcement (which for some reason was in Niko's angel mode), the passengers dropped down to the ground one after the other. When Haruyuki landed last, carrying Fuko's wheelchair, the massive tank was swallowed up in red light and vanished. A bright-red female avatar jumped forward from where the cockpit had been.

The drive from Umesato Junior High in Suginami across the city to Marunouchi finally over, the Red King, Scarlet Rain, thrust both arms out ahead of her. "Aaah, all those narrow roads!" she hissed at a stretch. "I really had to concentrate, dammit. We're taking the expressway home!"

"Whaaaat?! But there aren't any brakes!!" Haruyuki cried out, before hurrying to add, "A-and the expressway overpasses looked like they were crumbling all over the place. It's just, maybe they can't hold up a big vehicle, you know? I mean..."

"Between the two missions, there'll prob'ly be at least one Change," Niko replied evenly, hands clasped behind her head. "Or, like, I seriously wish we'd get one already. And it'd be the best if we got a fire type, like Lava or Scorched Earth."

"Huh? Why—? Oh! I get it. If it's a fire-related stage, Seiryu's power will weaken."

"Mm. But there's also the possibility of a water stage, though," Black Lotus said, turning her mirrored goggles up at the dark sky as she stood beside Niko. "We should be happy with the Century End stage. It doesn't rain in this one, at least. At any rate, if we're going to cross our fingers for a Change, I'd rather save our luck for the attack on Metatron."

"Right. A bit of a higher-level dark stage, and if we could, the best would be..." Haruyuki was still gripping the handles of the wheelchair where Fuko was sitting, and she quietly picked up where he left off:

"...The pinnacle of dark types, a Hell stage. That way, we'd be able to fight Metatron together with you, Corvus..."

"Mm, true...But even I can basically count on one hand the number of times I've seen a Hell stage in the Unlimited Neutral Field. We do have the option of waiting until the very last minute of our seven-day time limit, but the probability is fairly close to zero..."

"I'm sure it'll work out!" Chiyuri's bright voice broke the moment of silence that fell over them. "That's why Crow worked so hard to learn Optical Conduction! He'd knock Metatron's laser right back at the thing easy as pie, I'm sure of it!"

This is probably where I step in and say something like "Yeah! Leave it to me!" Even with this thought in his mind, what came out of Haruyuki's mouth was the usual "I'll do what I can."

But Pard slapped him on the shoulder, having come to stand behind him at some point. "'Kay. You can do it."

"R-right!"

Her tone was curt, but the older Burst Linker had always gently encouraged him, so Haruyuki turned to face her, wanting to let her know that he was genuinely committed to the act. But by the time he had taken a deep enough breath, Pard was already walking away. Long tail flicking, she moved on silent feet to the west side of the intersection, facing the towering Castle.

Haruyuki watched the slender, tough back of the leopard avatar and slowly expelled the air stored in his lungs. Right. This was not the time to get preoccupied with the Metatron fight. They had an objective to achieve before that one, one that required his complete focus:

The rescue of one of Nega Nebulus's Four Elements, Aqua Current, sealed away at the east gate of the Castle.

Haruyuki removed his hands from Fuko's wheelchair and clenched them into fists. He stood like that as he turned in a slow circle, carving his surroundings into his memory.

To the north, he could see the Tokyo fire department and the Japan Meteorological Agency, along with the overhead bridge of the expressway ring road.

To the east, Tokyo Station sat at the end of a broad road. Even in the Century End stage, the redbrick construction was maintained, but the walls were crumbling and scorched in places.

When he turned to the south, he found Hibiya Park, which they had passed only moments earlier, and the government buildings of Kasumigaseki. Was the thin iron tower soaring far off in the distance the old Tokyo Tower?

And then: To the west, there was the iron bridge spanning the sheer precipice of the bottomless ravine and the massive gate closed tight on the other side. The gate doors, likely thirty meters tall and wide, were also made of steel, but not a trace of rust or denting could be found on the dark surface. It appeared to be the only thing in the world of the Century End stage—which took post-apocalyptic as its theme—that refused to be corroded at all.

"The Castle...The east gate," Haruyuki murmured.

Moving to his right side, Kuroyukihime nodded softly. "Curren is locked away on the altar in front of that gate. We'll have a briefing now on the details of the mission, but just like with the south gate, I'll no doubt be asking you to play a critical role. It's cowardly of me to consistently rely on you as your parent and as your Legion Master, but I *am* counting on you, Haruyuki."

"That's— To start with, I'm the one who asked you all to come on this mission today."

"No, ever since Curren returned to the Legion, her rescue from the Castle has been an objective we needed to achieve as soon as possible. It's the same for the Metatron mission. The spread of the ISS kits has come to a point that's one step away from an epidemic. In fact, I think your insistence was the push I needed when I was hesitating." Kuroyukihime touched the flat side of the sword that was her left hand to Haruyuki's shoulder, and then brought her face mask very close.

"...To be honest," she murmured, "that fear inside me hasn't gone away. Will we not see fresh sacrifices against this opponent, the God Seiryu? Will we not confront some unexpected truth at Tokyo Midtown Tower? But at the same time, I also have faith. That no matter what the hardship, your silver wings will slice through it...for us."

"...Yes." He wanted to say so much more, but a hot lump had risen in his throat, and it was all he could do to push out that short answer. Instead, Haruyuki wrapped the fingers of his right hand gently around the tip of Kuroyukihime's left. He squeezed as hard as he dared—any harder, and he risked having his fingers chopped off by her Terminate Sword—and then managed to add a few more words: "It's okay. Whatever happens, I'll protect you. And everyone else."

Kuroyukihime's reply was to nod deeply and then lightly touch her head to Haruyuki's helmet.

Just this once, none of the others made an attempt to tease them or comment on the scene. The pair simply leaned against each other as they looked up at the Castle gate.

After a few seconds, Kuroyukihime stood up once more and turned back to the others behind them. She reached out and opened her Instruct menu, and then after a glance at a window only she could see, her clear voice rang out:

"It's been exactly thirty minutes since we entered the Unlimited Neutral Field. In the real world, 1.8 seconds have passed. Aqua Current is scheduled to dive ten seconds after we did, which works out to two hours and forty-six minutes on this side. In other words, we have two hours and sixteen minutes left to wait. First, we'll take a fifteen-minute break before we start the mission brief."

"Wellll then, I'll just go poke around Tokyo Station—," Niko started.

"No!" Kuroyukihime barked instantly, frighteningly. "There's a portal there, and Aurora Oval territory is on the other side of the tracks. Worst-case scenario, if you run into Thorn's people, the situation will instantly become a major hassle."

"Aah. Yeah, I guess so." Niko nodded meekly. Apparently, even she wasn't too interested in actively engaging the Purple King, Purple Thorn. "Nothing to be done about that. So how 'bout you show me around the Castle, Professor?"

"Wh-what?! Why me?!" Takumu immediately panicked, like someone had just dumped a bucket of cold water on him.

"You didn't actually forget, didja?" Niko stared at him with her green eye lenses. "How I was there for all that Incarnate training of yours? I'll say this right now—I've never even done that kinda special lesson for my own Prominence kids!"

"I—I didn't forget! Of course not! But how can I show you around when we can't go inside…?"

"Just what we can see from here's fine. The east gate there, it has a different name with some kinda historical trivia in the real world, yeah?" Niko pointed an adorable hand at the steel gate, and Takumu and the others followed with their eyes.

Now that she mentioned it, the four gates of the Castle did correspond to the gates built to the north, east, south, and west of the former Edo Castle—the Imperial Palace in the real world. And just like the Hanzomon gate in the west and the Sakuradamon gate in the south, the east must also have had a name.

"Um." When all eyes were back on Takumu, the blue duel avatar that served as the Legion's staff officer cleared his throat once before explaining, slightly awkwardly, "The Castle's east gate is called Sakashitamon in the real world. It was one of the inner gates of Edo Castle, and where, in January 1862, six Mito Domain soldiers attacked the *roju* elder Nobumasa Ando."

Haruyuki's brain was about to reject the sudden school vibe in the air and tune out, but at the same time, Takumu's speech jogged a part of his memory, and he twisted his upper body at a strange angle and groaned.

"Um, um, um. I feel like I've heard that before…You know, that— Right, the Sakashitamon Incident!" he shouted, having miraculously succeeded in replaying the memory.

"Anyone would remember that when they heard Sakashitamon." Chiyuri immediately came back with a merciless retort. "So then, question! What was the reason for the attack?"

"Uh! Um, that was, like, they couldn't stand the *roju* Ando, so a PK—"

"Details, please! The reason they couldn't stand him?"

"Uhhhh. Um. Pretty sure…" Haruyuki hadn't been expecting a test on Japanese history here, and he did his best to pull up what little half-baked knowledge he had. "That's— Ando signed a treaty with the US and totally persecuted the imperialists who were against it—"

"*Bzzzzt!*" Chiyuri made an "incorrect" buzzer noise.

"So close, Corvus." Fuko turned toward Haruyuki, wheelchair and all, holding up her index finger and grinning. "It was the *tairo* elder Ii Naosuke who carried out the Ansei Purge. Incidentally, he was also attacked by the Mito Domain soldiers, but that was at the south gate over there, the so-called Sakuradamon Incident. That happened in 1860, so two years before the Sakashitamon Incident."

"Oh! I-it did…So then why was Ando attacked?"

"To strengthen the shaky feudal system, Nobumasa Ando recommended uniting the Imperial court with the shogunate. As a symbol of this, he had the younger sister of Emperor Komei, Kazunomiya, married off to the fourteenth shogun, Iemochi

Tokugawa. They say that this was what made the lordless, imperialist Mito samurai attack."

The cache memory in Haruyuki's brain had just barely enough capacity for this string of proper nouns, but he managed to process it somehow and bobbed his head up and down. "I—I get it. There were six samurai who attacked, right? And the defense—I mean, the samurai guarding Ando, how many of them were there?"

Takumu cleared his throat before answering. "I guess forty-five samurai from the Iwakitaira domain were guarding him. Iwakitaira was Nobumasa's territory in what's now the southern part of Fukushima prefecture."

Haruyuki automatically converted this explanation into forty-five members of the Legion Iwakitaira, but he kept that to himself, and instead crossed his arms and groaned. "Whoa, six against forty-five, huh? So what's happening in the boss figh—I mean, attack?"

"The Mito samurai were all cut down and killed; there were no deaths among the Iwakitaira samurai. Nobumasa Ando's back was hurt, but he escaped into the Castle and was safe."

"Hmm. He was…" Of course, Haruyuki didn't know enough to root for one side or the other when it came to samurai who had crossed swords in that place in the real world a hundred eighty-five years earlier. But listening to Takumu, he couldn't help conflating the two. The eight Burst Linkers taking on a powerful Super-class Enemy and the six samurai who were cut down in the distant past.

"Aah, honestly, why are you so easy to read, Haru?" Chiyuri sounded suddenly exasperated, and Haruyuki flinched. The yellow-green witch-type avatar was shaking her triangle hat in a way that suggested she was rolling her eyes.

"Wh-what do you mean, easy to read?"

"We're also going to be struck down and killed. You were brooding or something like that, weren't you?"

"Unh!"

"Now, look, this is totally different! We didn't come to assassinate a *roju*; we came to help Curren! And you were fine when you got shoved into the Castle, so don't go getting freaked out now in front of the gate!"

He did feel her logic was a little forced, but when his childhood friend rattled on at him with her usual vigor, Haruyuki inevitably agreed with an "I get it." Nodding deeply, he clenched his right hand. "Right, no matter how you look at it, we're in the right this time! If we could somehow defeat Seiryu with justice power, then our points would—"

"Don't get carried away!"

Thmp! The edge of Choir Chime was jabbed into his side, and Haruyuki fell silent, leaving the others to sigh in unison.

"Now that preparations for the upcoming final exams are complete, how about we get to the strategy meeting?" Kuroyukihime said as if to change the subject, clearing her throat lightly and moving to the mouth of the bridge. "You're ready, yes?"

The voices that chimed their assent were a little lackluster, and Haruyuki was convinced it was because of the words in the Black King's speech that every student had long ago learned to dread.

The waiting time of two hours and fifteen minutes, which had seemed ridiculously long when announced, slipped by in the blink of an eye with a thorough briefing and a run-through of the mission.

Kuroyukihime checked the total dive time display on her Instruct menu once more before turning around. "All right. Fifteen minutes until the mission begins. Curren should be fairly precise with the timing, but an error of 0.1 seconds in the real world expands to a hundred seconds over here. Which is to say, we need to add a window of two minutes or so to our calculations."

In the mission to rescue Ardor Maiden twelve days earlier, once they had finished their preparations on the Unlimited Neutral Field side, Takumu had left through the nearest portal and told Utai in the real world to accelerate.

But this time, they had fixed Aqua Current's—Akira Himi's—dive time in advance. So if, for some reason, the advance party's charge onto the steel bridge had been delayed, Akira would have been killed by the God Seiryu immediately after she appeared. Fortunately, thanks to Niko's "taxi," they had arrived at the east gate without incident and completed their preparations without delay, but now, the real fight started. Haruyuki focused his mind so as not to miss a single thing Kuroyukihime said.

"The last time, after going up against Suzaku twice, we learned that the Gods have apparently been given an AI more advanced than Legend-class Enemies. It's not necessarily the case that they continually target whoever is doing them the most damage, and they also move as if to deliberately outwit us. We might be put into a situation that we didn't cover in our simulation. In that case, all we can do is play it by ear, but make sure you place top priority on your own withdrawal. We must at least avoid anyone else getting sealed away."

The Black King's voice was calm, but Haruyuki noticed a faint hint of struggle in her last sentence.

When Kuroyukihime and Fuko had nearly been roasted alive in the previous Castle rescue mission, they had tried to sacrifice themselves to save Haruyuki and Utai. That act was a clear contradiction to what she was saying now. Most likely, Kuroyukihime had again already resolved in her heart that she alone would prioritize the withdrawal of her companions.

But he was sure it was the same for Fuko and Utai and Takumu and Chiyuri and Niko and Pard. It was precisely because they all shared the conviction that they absolutely could not abandon a friend that they were gathered together there in the first place. That feeling was a Burst Linker's greatest strength.

"Yeah, yeah, got it, Lotus!" Scarlet Rain said, sitting on an oil drum instead of a chair and kicking both legs up and down. "Basic idea, we go charging in, all raaah, get Aqua Current, and then we all run away, like whoa, right? It's only five hundred meters each way. Piece of cake!"

"You say *only*, Rain, but when you're running, five hundred meters is really far. The return trip is a kilometer."

"So what's a kilometer! I mean, at my school marathon, the grade sixes ran *three* kilometers! Aah, seriously, I'm getting tired just thinking about it."

"Don't underestimate us! Our school's marathon is five kilometers! That's a distance the word *tired* doesn't begin to express!" The kings' exchange was sliding further and further off track.

"Niko, Kuroyukihime," Chiyuri interjected, exasperated. "I run that far-*ish* every day at practice."

"...Are you serious? You trying to die, Lime Bell?"

"...I apologize for the low-level argument." Kuroyukihime dipped her head and then straightened up to look at everyone, easing the slightly tense pre-mission atmosphere, albeit only slightly. She slowly blinked her bluish-purple eye lenses, then spoke in a voice that was calm yet full of her strong will.

"Just as Rain said, the mission itself is simple. I believe it's possible to break through Seiryu's powerful attack with this battle formation. Ten minutes to show time. Let's take our starting positions."

2

What was the true nature of an Enhanced Armament?

Posed with this question, the majority of low-level Burst Link-ers would likely respond that they were an enhancement of attack power. And that was certainly not wrong; gun- and sword-type Enhanced Armaments dramatically increased the attack power of a duel avatar and expanded the range of battle tactics.

But for Burst Linkers who had reached midlevel or higher, who had built up experience through wins and losses in countless duels in the Accelerated World, the true advantages of Enhanced Armaments were seen in defense.

And this was because a defensive Enhanced Armament was not a mere enhancement of defensive ability. In fact, there was one very simple factor that made this so, but because of that sim-plicity, it was not so easy to recognize:

While an Enhanced Armament was taking the enemy's attacks, the health gauge of the user did not decrease.

To look at it another way, this was equivalent to doubling or tripling the health gauge. In the Accelerated World, where, as a general rule, the means to recover health did not exist, hit points were not particularly remarkable, but they were the most impor-tant parameter.

Of course, that said, just because someone had strong additional armor didn't necessarily make them the strongest. Armor-type Enhanced Armaments were heavy and interfered with movement, so without mastery of it, its use only made that person a target. They needed either the power to be able to move lightly while wrapped in armor or the firepower to shoot and win even when motionless.

The ultimate example of the former was the armor that had introduced Haruyuki to overwhelming battle power, the Armor of Catastrophe, aka Chrome Disaster. And the ultimate example of the latter was the Immobile Fortress, Scarlet Rain.

"Here we...goooooooooo!!"

The Red King's roar, replete with her indomitable spirit, fired the first shot of the mission to rescue Aqua Current, which finally started at 12:20:10 PM, June 30, 2047, real-world time.

The twelve wheels of the re-summoned Enhanced Armament, the armored Dreadnought, spun fiercely, leaving burn marks on the road of the Century End stage. The treads of the tires finally bit into the pavement, and the massive vehicle lurched forward, tearing up the asphalt as it went.

For their starting point, they'd decided on a place about three hundred meters from the entrance to the bridge in front of the east gate of the Castle. They'd cleared away the oil drums and chunks of concrete beforehand, so there were no objects to get in the way of driving. Moving forward in a straight line, the massive crimson carriage picked up speed along the improvised long jump track.

Niko was, naturally, in the cockpit, but the seven other members of the team were not on the roof. Rather, they were standing on the barrels of the laser guns mounted on both sides of the vehicle, holding on tightly. On the left: Kuroyukihime, Haruyuki, Takumu. On the right: Pard, Chiyuri, Fuko, Utai.

And the reason they were not all riding on the roof was...

"Missiles prepaaaaare to fire!" Niko yelled again, and the armor plating on the top of the vehicle popped open in four places.

From inside, countless missiles steadily rose. The tank/truck continued to accelerate fiercely as it moved into attack position, and the black steel bridge grew closer with every breath.

The thirty-meter-wide, five-hundred-meter-long bridge spanning the bottomless ravine was territory guarded by the God Seiryu. The battlefield was too small for the massive body of the Super-class Enemy. It went without saying that siege attacks would have been difficult, but even just slipping around to get behind it was likely impossible. Thus, when they went to rescue Ardor Maiden, the strategy they came up with had Haruyuki flying at super-high speed with a boost from Fuko's Gale Thruster, to shoot past the God Suzaku immediately after it appeared. Although things had gone well up to that point, he had been flying so fast that he hadn't been able to turn around, leading to his and Utai's plunge into the Castle.

Learning from this experience, they had decided to charge forward on the ground this time, but the Dreadnought was similarly unable to turn on a moment's notice. In fact, the armored trailer didn't even have any brakes. But Niko continued to fearlessly stomp on the accelerator, and just as they were about to cross onto the bridge, a loud voice rang out for a third time.

"Hold on tight! Thrusters, oooooooon!!"

Hrrum! An explosive sound echoed through the air, and a remarkably intense sense of acceleration came over Haruyuki. The rocket motors equipped at the rear of the trailer had been ignited.

And then the front tires crossed the boundary between the asphalt road and the steel bridge.

It felt to Haruyuki like the color of the air had changed. Even though he still couldn't see anything ahead of them, an excessively concentrated sense of presence—probably what Niko called *information pressure*—bounced off the armor of his entire body.

"...Here it comes!" Kuroyukihime shouted from her position directly in front of him.

Up ahead on the other side of the bridge, in the air above the square altar that stood in front of the Castle's east gate, a swaying blue light was flickering. Almost like the shimmering of water, it grew larger and larger with each passing second. Finally, several ripples spread outward from two clear, foreboding lights shining in the center. Then he heard the pounding rush of water, and a massive figure danced up from the surface of the phantom lake.

A head with countless fangs and four horns. A neck covered in diamond-shaped scales followed, while front legs writhed in space. The long torso twisted, claws appeared on its back legs, and a sharp whiplike tail drew out in a large arc. Bristles with a golden luster stood on end upon its back, all the way from its head down to the tail. Lastly, from there, four pairs of small, evenly spaced wings stretched out.

Neither Western- nor Eastern-style but still a magnificent dragon. Perhaps because of the phosphorescence enveloping its body, even in the gloom of the Century End stage its massive form shone a deep, vivid lapis lazuli. And the two eyes all the more so, like polished eternal ice.

Having finally taken form, the God Seiryu opened its maw wide and let loose a howl like thunder. The air trembled, and Haruyuki had to grit his teeth to withstand the pressure.

Of the eight people riding on the tank, the six members of Nega Nebulus had experience with another Super-class Enemy, Suzaku. But this was the first encounter for the two members of Prominence.

Haruyuki couldn't see Niko in the cockpit or Blood Leopard on the opposite side of the vehicle, but with this terrifying figure before them, for a few moments at least, he was sure they would both be stunned—

"Take this, you snake jerk! Missiles! Launch aaaaaallll!!"

A shout rang out as if to dispel all of Haruyuki's concerns, and the area above the trailer was suddenly filled with light and sound. The flames of countless shots fired lit up the gloom, and the small missiles whistled through the air one after the other.

They ascended for a time before changing angles and plummeting toward the massive body of the Enemy.

Orange balls of fire blossomed in succession and swallowed up the patrolling Seiryu. Multiple explosions shook the bridge and the tank racing along on top of it.

"Everyone! Move to the roof!" Kuroyukihime shouted without waiting for the exploding flames four hundred meters ahead to subside.

The group kicked at the guns and leapt to the top of the vehicle. The missile pods were still open, so their footing was a bit uneven, but not to the point where they couldn't stand up.

"Long distance attack, start!"

"Right!" Haruyuki called, readying himself alongside everyone else. He thrust his right hand forward over the missile pod cover and braced it with his left.

But the very first to launch was Cyan Pile's special attack. "Lightning Cyan Spike!!"

The iron spike, now in the form of superheated plasma, shot forward with incredible speed and was quickly swallowed up by the silhouette blinking in and out of view within the flames of the explosion. It had only cut a small hole in the Shinjuku bridge girder, but against the armor of a Super-class Enemy opponent, its proud penetrating power should have produced real results.

Hot on his heels, Haruyuki pulled back the silver overlay in his right hand. The instant the light lance was produced, he drew it back as far as it could go and shouted the technique name: "Laser Javelin!!"

For Haruyuki, who had no flying weapons, this Incarnate technique was his sole means of long-range attack. It was an adaptation of his midrange attack, Laser Lance, but because it had been formed with fairly coercive logic, its accuracy was a little off. As the lance whistled through the air, its trajectory was a faint spiral rather than a straight line. He was just lucky the Enemy was so huge; it looked like the lance would hit somewhere on the tail.

Here, the missile launch was finally finished, and on the other side of the curtain of black smoke, Haruyuki felt Seiryu starting to move once more. But not about to let that happen, Utai turned her longbow Flame Caller toward the sky. "Flame Torrents!!"

The clear call was accompanied by a flame arrow winding its way upward. At the peak of its arc, it split into dozens of arrows that became a torrential downpour of flames raining down on the Enemy. The countless small explosions that immediately popped up didn't compare to the missiles in range, but the burn time was longer. The massive blue dragon writhed in irritation within the blaze.

"Aaaaaah!" A powerful battle cry sounded over the roar of the tank, echoing through the air. Kuroyukihime, standing a row ahead of Haruyuki, brought a crimson overlay into a hand brandished high above her. The long sword turned from onyx to ruby as she braced it above her shoulder. "Vorpal Strike!"

Her right hand shot forward at nearly light speed, and a ray of light the color of blood jetted out. Instantaneously piercing a distance of over two hundred meters, it plunged into Seiryu's chest, still caught up in flames. Hit hard, the massive body shuddered, and the creature's metallic shriek echoed through the field.

"How about thiiiiis!" Niko shouted once more. *"Heat Blast Saturatioooooon!!"*

Klank! The main guns on both sides of the vehicle turned upward, and a faint ruby-red light leaked from the wide barrels. This quickly increased in brightness before becoming a cross-shaped beam, and—

Knnrrrkeeeee! The sound of resonance was earsplitting as the hugely thick laser fired.

Likely double the scale of the normal shot that had evaporated Silver Crow a week earlier during his special training to acquire the Theoretical Mirror ability, and released simultaneously from both left and right guns, the lasers merged a few dozen meters out to produce a massive energy lance that was more like a pillar of light. Haruyuki had once witnessed this technique blow away the government building in Shinjuku with one shot.

The Red King's second special attack, currently considered the most powerful long-range attack in the Accelerated World, dug into the spot in Seiryu's chest that the Black King's special attack had pierced and swelled up into a bright-red ball of light, before bringing about an explosion so large it nearly shook both heaven and earth. The pillar of flames stretched up higher and higher, reaching the distant sky and coloring the bottoms of the hanging black clouds red.

Counting the initial missile attack, the six successive shots had all been powerful blows—special attacks and Incarnate techniques. Seiryu might have been one of the strongest Enemies in the Accelerated World, but it had to have taken at least that much damage. And maybe it would even be stunned for a while. With these thoughts rolling around in his mind, Haruyuki peered into the flames and smoke.

Displayed above the massive silhouette was a five-tier health gauge the same as Suzaku's. With their approach, the first tier was shaved down by nearly 30 percent. But.

"Unnh." A low groan slipped out of Haruyuki. The gauge they had worked so hard to decrease was recovered from left to right before his eyes.

This was something they had run through in the advance simulation. The Super-class Enemies that guarded the four gates of the Castle were, in a certain sense, four creatures as one. One was injured, and any of the other three not engaged in a fight would heal it. Which meant that if you wanted to defeat the Four Gods, the only thing to do was attack all four simultaneously and defeat them simultaneously. The difficulty of this was clear, even without bringing up the tragedy of the former Nega Nebulus.

Thus, their current strategy didn't even pay lip service to the idea of subjugating Seiryu. The attack was, at most, a means of drawing its ire—which Haruyuki knew in his mind—but even so, he was still mildly shocked that the damage induced by a team that included two Kings giving it everything they had could be so easily erased.

"That attack didn't even take out one gauge," Takumu muttered in a strained voice from beside him.

"We don't have time for disappointment, Crow, Pile." It was Fuko behind them who spoke. Her voice was normally soft and gentle, but of course, at that moment, it was sharp and tight. "The counterattack's coming. Everyone, hide behind the armor panels!"

This instruction was joined by a roar like thunder. From the black smoke lingering in the air above the altar now two hundred meters ahead, a blue mass shot forward, ferocious. The sapphire eyes seethed with rage, and the long jaw was wide open.

Krshk! From beyond the countless fangs came a pale beam of light—no, a stream of water. It was one of the specialized attacks Aqua Current had warned them about in advance: Water Breath. The power that lay in that super-high-pressure jet of water would dig into even the superior armor of green-type avatars.

Haruyuki ducked down and hid behind the iron plate in front of him—the open cover of the missile pod. Kuroyukihime, Takumu, Chiyuri, and the others all did the same, while Fuko alone continued to stand resolutely behind them.

She raised the palm of her right hand in front of her and shouted, "Wind Veil!!"

The sound echoed deeply, and the green wind that began to swirl in the center of her palm enveloped the entire tank.

And then Seiryu's Breath attack, which was expanding in diameter to similarly swallow the tank, slammed into them. Still kneeling, Haruyuki turned his gaze upward.

The green dome given shape by the swirling wind knocked the countless jets of streaming water away, scattering them as white mist. But the defensive wind's force and speed were weakening, and Fuko let out a small grunt behind him. Her raised palm shook as though it might not be able to withstand the pressure, her body itself was pushed back, and she finally dropped to her knees.

Haruyuki's field of view was dyed white. The dragon's attack had broken Fuko's Incarnate shield and was pouring down onto the trailer.

The high-frequency vibration nearly shattered his virtual eardrums. The vehicle shook and shuddered. Several hundred jets of water dug into every part of Dreadnought's thick armor. If it were an avatar's body subjected to this attack, their health gauge would have dropped with terrifying force.

However.

"Heh! Giving me a high-pressure wash for free, pretty generous, you snake in the boot!!"

The tank did indeed slow down, but even still, it pushed valiantly forward against the gale while Niko taunted Seiryu.

Her voice was not colored by any kind of pain.

Because, while an Enhanced Armament was taking an attack, its owner's health gauge did not drop.

It had been Niko herself, the owner of the vehicle, who had proposed this strategy of using the armored truck as an assault vehicle to get as close as possible to the altar, leaving the armor to bear the brunt of Seiryu's attacks. Nega Nebulus had hesitated about a battle strategy that was the equivalent of using a trailer and then tossing it aside, but the Red King had been nonchalant. *"You guys don't get the true nature of Enhanced Armament, you know?"*

—*Thank you, Niko. We're not going to waste this spirit of yours! No way!* Haruyuki cried in his heart as he held up the cover of the missile pod with both hands. The thick steel shuddered, telling him that Seiryu's Breath attack was still digging holes in it.

But perhaps, thanks to Fuko's Incarnate technique deflecting some percentage of the force, his impromptu defensive wall withstood the entire attack without being pierced. The trailer once again picked up speed, and the Super-class Enemy plunged forward in the sky above. The distance between them finally was pushed below a hundred meters.

According to their advance information, the flip side of Seiryu having the most diverse specialized attacks of the Four Gods was that the frequency of physical attacks was low. Naturally, that didn't mean it was zero, and a blow from those sharp fangs or claws or tail was a threat, but the armor of the trailer was still holding, albeit full of holes. It would protect the team a little longer.

But above all else, the most terrifying thing once they crossed into the midrange distance was—

Haruyuki's brain had made it this far when Kuroyukihime barked from the front, "It's time! Five seconds to go…Two, one, zero!"

A mere three seconds after the countdown.

A faint sky-blue light shuddered into existence in the center of the altar, which he could now see clearly up ahead.

The duel avatar appearance effect.

Blue light expanded and then coalesced, producing a slender silhouette.

A clear, watery film enveloping the entire body. Four streams of water, like plumes carving out arcs through the air. One of Nega Nebulus's Four Elements, water, Aqua Current.

She matched their timing with fearsome accuracy, yet was standing in the Unlimited Neutral Field for the first time in two years and ten months.

Haruyuki forced himself to pull his gaze away from the avatar glittering so beautifully in the light of the watch fires that sat on the four sides of the square altar. What he needed to be looking at now was the God Seiryu. During the mission to rescue Ardor Maiden, the God Suzaku had turned around at this point and swooped in to attack Utai on the altar.

But the massive lapis lazuli dragon didn't slacken its pace as it closed in on the tank. It was fairly angry about the sudden succession of six massive attacks that had carved away its health gauge and the fact that its Breath had been defended—or rather, its aggression had increased.

But that was exactly what they wanted. The success or failure of the plan rested on whether or not the attacking team, with Kuroyukihime at the center, would be able to continue to lure Seiryu in until the very end.

The massive dragon had gotten close enough that it almost covered the sky, and now its four horns shone with a pale light.

Several sparks raced through the black clouds in the sky above. Coming together in a number of places, they flashed with remarkable brightness—

"Splash Stinger!!" Takumu shouted, throwing his head back. Needle missiles were launched one after another from the holes that opened up in the armor on his chest.

At nearly the same time, purple bolts of lightning zigzagged down from the sky with a thunderous roar. This was Seiryu's second specialized attack—Thunder Blast. The vertical missile pod covers on the tank that had been their shields thus far wouldn't shelter them from a lightning strike from above.

But all of the lightning was drawn into Takumu's missiles, bringing about countless explosions overhead.

However, they couldn't completely negate the lightning's energy, and purple light pierced the flames of the blasts, stretching out toward the team of avatars. But perhaps knocked off course, the purple streaks fell onto the steel bridge instead. One bolt made a direct hit on the tank and traveled through the surface of the armor, causing one of the tires to burst—but the members of the strike force were all still uninjured.

Once Seiryu carried out a specialized attack, there appeared to be a brief charging time before the next one. If they could slip directly under it during this opening, Haruyuki was sure they could reach the altar where Current was waiting.

The Enemy howled as if to negate this hope, and its massive body bent abruptly to build up power. The tail twisted into an S and came down so fast, it almost couldn't be seen. The tip scraped the steel bridge's surface, sending sparks flying, and then kept going to slam into the front of the tank.

If Niko hadn't yanked the wheel to one side, the cockpit might have been crushed. They just barely managed to avert that tragedy, but the tail, like an iron pillar, came down hard on the front right of the vehicle, and the tires on the right side began to spin helplessly as they rose into the air.

"*Dammit.*" Cursing, Niko tried desperately to rally, but the vehicle tilted farther and farther to one side with each breath, leaving Haruyuki and the others on the roof unable to stand and scrambling to grab hold of the armor plates. If the trailer fell onto its side, more than a few would get pulled in and take some fairly serious damage.

Niko was probably thinking the same thing. From the speakers came a regretful voice. *"It's no use. I'm gonna send it back for now! Everyone, get ready to jump off! ...Enhanced Armament, release!!"*

Simultaneous with the voice command, the trailer, on the verge of toppling over sideways, started to break apart. It hadn't been destroyed, but rather returned to storage on Niko's orders. The ease of bringing it in and out was a significant advantage of Enhanced Armaments, but once it was released, it couldn't be summoned again until a cooldown time set for each armament had passed.

The disassembled laser guns and missile pods and all the other parts faded and disappeared, melting into the air. The team members on top lost their foothold and Niko was ejected from the cockpit, all of them thrown onto the steel bridge's surface.

"Aaaah!" —Chiyuri.

"Whoa!" —Takumu.

Haruyuki instantly deployed his wings. He scooped up Lime Bell with his right hand and Cyan Pile with his left before carefully decelerating in midair and setting them down on the road surface. The others managed to land without difficulty or damage on their own. The deft grace displayed by even Utai, a total long-distance type, was no doubt because of her experience with Fuko throwing her mercilessly through the air.

The commander of the mission, Kuroyukihime, had no sooner confirmed they were all okay than she was shouting in a stifled voice, "Raker, go! I'll hold things down here!"

"Understood. I'll leave this to you then." As if pushing back a momentary hesitation, Fuko nodded and jumped into the wheelchair she had summoned at some point. The silver wheels glittered faintly, and then her elegant Enhanced Armament set off like a rocket toward the altar a hundred meters ahead. Her speed—accelerating using Incarnate—far surpassed normal running. The tracks left on the surface of the bridge burned red, thin trails of smoke rising up.

In the previous mission, Sky Raker's role had been to catapult Haruyuki, but this time, she was charged with rescuing Aqua Current on her own.

Master, we're counting on you! Haruyuki shouted in his mind as he took just a moment to watch the wheelchair race off. Up ahead, Current had already stepped down from the altar and broken into a run. Only a few seconds before they made contact.

Then.

Haruyuki heard a sonorous voice directly in the center of his mind. Or he felt like he did anyway.

—Tiny transient creatures.
—For what purpose do you disturb my sleep?

Reflexively, he flung his head back. His eyes were drawn to those of the Super-class Enemy cruising through the sky—almost covering it—glittering like sapphires. For a moment, he braced himself, thinking *that attack* was finally coming, but he was wrong.

A cold halo gushed forth from the eyes of the massive dragon, in which he could feel an unfathomable intelligence and will.

Suddenly, Haruyuki's entire body stiffened—no, froze. A

snowy-white frost fell onto Silver Crow's metallic armor, and he could no longer move even a fingertip, much less his wings. Panicking, he flicked his eyes from side to side, but the others were similarly frozen.

He didn't have to think back to the strategy meeting; this was a completely unknown attack. He had been aware their advance information wouldn't necessarily cover all of Seiryu's abilities, but it was entirely unexpected that they would get hit with such a powerful technique to hinder movement. Not only could Haruyuki not move, he couldn't even speak—meaning it was impossible to break the ice with a special attack. And the frost cage showed no sign of shattering, no matter how much he pushed against it.

Above them, Seiryu barely bothered to give its new ice sculptures a cool glance before it turned its head, as if having lost interest. Turned—toward the west side of the bridge and the altar there.

Looking as far to the side as he possibly could without shifting his head, he saw the figures of Fuko and Akira about to touch hands. In their plan, once Sky Raker had recovered Aqua Current, she would use Gale Thruster and escape to the sky. She would then ascend to an altitude of three hundred meters, near her flight maximum, overtake Seiryu, and land on the other side of the bridge.

But that strategy was possible only as long as the attack team continued to draw Seiryu's fire. Recharging Gale Thruster's energy gauge took a long time, so if they were beat back shortly after taking off, it wouldn't just be Akira; Fuko would also end up in Unlimited EK on the far side of the bridge.

Almost as though tracing Haruyuki's fretful line of thinking, Seiryu open its jaw wide.

The Water Breath attack. If they took a direct hit from those super-high-pressure water jets—essentially diamond needles—Raker with her thin armor, and probably Current as well, would not be able to avoid instant death.

＊　　　＊　　　＊

...I will not let you do that!!

Once more, a shout echoed in the back of his mind. But this time, it was not the Enemy, but rather the intense willpower of Utai Shinomiya—Ardor Maiden, shrine keeper of the conflagration—shooting forth.

A ring of red flames expanded out from her body to envelop them all. The fierce heat instantly melted the frost that bound their avatars. An Incarnate technique—wait, no, not a technique. The overlay from the manifestation of a powerful imagination had itself turned into flames.

Naturally, a fine tuning of that temperature seemed impossible, and at the same time as they melted the frost, the flames sliced away a tiny bit of Haruyuki's health gauge. But he forgot both the heat and the pain. Freed from his icy state, Haruyuki thrust his right hand into the air with all his might.

"Laser Lance!!"

"Radiant Beat!!" Niko's voice rang out at exactly the same time.

The lance of light from Haruyuki's right hand and the fist of fire from Niko's shot upward, striking Seiryu's lower jaw while it was just about to shoot its Water Breath. The damage they did was paltry, but they succeeded in closing its mouth with the impact, just barely interrupting the attack. White water vapor spurted out from the gaps between fangs clamped forcibly together.

And then a pale-blue light flashed ferociously right in front of the altar:

The firing of the boosters.

Aqua Current in her arms, Sky Raker ascended, carving out a brilliant arc in the night sky. With an intense acceleration befitting her nickname of ICBM, they immediately plunged through the black clouds of the Century End stage and dyed them blue for an instant before disappearing.

"...All right!" Haruyuki quietly cried out, clenching his right hand into a fist.

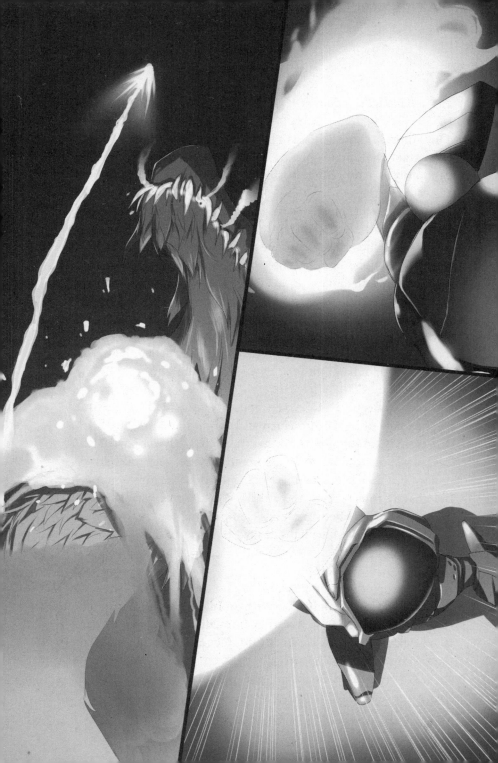

Although they had been in danger several times already, this was an infinitely smoother rescue than Ardor Maiden's had been. But given the team they were fighting with, Haruyuki could say that the success of the first half of the mission was a foregone conclusion. The problems started now—Whether or not Fuko and Akira could safely escape to the other side of the bridge while the rest on the ground occupied Seiryu's attention. It would all be for nothing if they came out of this with another person sealed away while they were pulling out.

"Good! Everyone! Fall back!"

At Kuroyukihime's instruction, the group started running to the east, all the while keeping the Enemy overhead in their field of view. Despite the fact that they had so far defended against the God Seiryu's specialized attacks three times, it still silently twisted its long body above them, maintaining its hate at a fixed value. Or so it looked.

...Is it letting us get away? Maybe the Four Gods have personality differences...Fiery Suzaku was easily angered, but watery Seiryu is surprisingly calm...Or something?

This thought suddenly popped up in Haruyuki's mind as he ran.

It was immediately after this that he heard once more what seemed to be the Enemy's voice. A voice that was quiet like the calm surface of a pool, reminiscent of a woman somehow, and cold like the polar regions.

—*I tire of this sport.*
—*Small ones, may you fall into a long sleep in our garden.*

The God pulled its long tail back as forcefully as it did when it knocked the armored truck over. But Haruyuki and his friends had already put more than twenty meters between themselves and the Enemy. No matter how he looked at it, they weren't close enough to be hit by a direct physical attack.

The tail was brought down so quickly, it blurred, and what it hit was not the seven Burst Linkers, but rather the iron bridge itself. *Gwaaaan!* The howl of the impact roared through the air, and the hard plates of the bridge heaved and surged. The shock wave rippling outward instantly swallowed up the running Burst Linkers and made even the hovering Kuroyukihime stagger.

No one fell, but for about half a second, they were all immobile, stunned. Not letting this chance slip away, Seiryu's horns glittered brilliantly, calling up ominous sparks in the black clouds above.

"Ngh…" Takumu intently braced both legs and threw his upper body back. But an instant before the missiles that served as lightning rods could be launched, several streaks of the accumulating electrical energy turned into purple lightning and shot out of the sky.

—No!

Reacting instinctively, Haruyuki vibrated the wings on his back with everything he had. They had to at least prevent everyone there from being struck by lightning. While Seiryu's specialized attack Thunder Blast did do damage, it also contained a de-buff that caused the entire body to go numb; a direct hit rendered the target unable to move for a period of time. According to their plan, Cyan Pile's Splash Stinger was supposed to knock the lightning off course, but if their luck was bad and someone did take a direct hit, then the others were to pick up the slack until that person recovered. But if they were all paralyzed, then of course that wouldn't work. In the worst case, they might even all be wiped out in the next attack.

—Better just me than that!

With his wings, Silver Crow was the only one who could jump after being thrown off-balance by the shock wave. Mustering all the propulsive force he could to take off, he threw both hands out, and the five bolts of lightning shooting down from the sky were all drawn to Crow's metallic armor.

"Ngah!"

The instant the bolts struck his body, a pure shock that went beyond the sensations of heat or pain pierced Haruyuki's consciousness. The world was dyed solid white, and he could no longer see the stage or the Enemy. All that existed within his field of view was his own health gauge. It had been basically full, but it was now dropping with alarming speed. Given that his armor was silver, the most conductive of the metals, Crow had always been weak to electrical attacks, but even allowing for that, the force with which his gauge was decreasing was impossible. No, this was on the level of instant death damage—

"Citron Caaaaaall!!"

From off in the distance, he just barely heard the resolute voice of his childhood friend. Glittering green particles danced through his vision and burned white. The steep drop in his health gauge slowed and stopped just barely before it disappeared completely. Then it jumped back up to the right, and he returned to the state he'd been in before being hit with the lightning bolts. Lime Bell's special attack, Citron Call Mode I, had rewound Silver Crow's status a few seconds and healed the damage—or rather, *made it as though it had never happened.*

He'd avoided sudden death, but that didn't take away the stunning shock of the lightning, and Haruyuki dropped out of the sky, white smoke trailing from his entire body. Cyan Pile's sturdy arms caught him and grabbed hold tightly. The bolts of lightning Haruyuki hadn't been able to completely draw into him had apparently all missed the mark.

"Pile!" It was, of course, Black Lotus yelling. "Keep running! Everyone else, cover Pile!"

Doing as he was told, Takumu started to run, still with Haruyuki in his arms. Blue eye lenses shone ruefully on the other side of the face mask in front of Haruyuki. "Sorry, Haru. I was supposed to be taking care of the lightning."

"It's...oka...not so ba..." Haruyuki somehow managed to make his numb mouth move.

Then, in the sky above, Seiryu lurched forward. Chasing after the seven Burst Linkers, it raised its tail up high once more. It was going for another hit with the attack-plus-shockwave combo.

"As if we would fall for the same trick twice!" Kuroyukihime's voice was uncompromising.

Haruyuki hurriedly lifted his head, wondering what she was planning to do. He saw her plunge the tip of her right leg into the bridge as a pivot to whirl around and charge at Seiryu behind them.

"Y...you can't, Kuroyukihime!" Haruyuki cried, finally able to move his mouth again, and jumped out of Takumu's arms without thinking. Staggering, he spread his wings and was on the verge of taking off when a small palm stopped him.

"Trust her," Niko murmured. "She's your parent."

With no choice, he put a halt to his flight and followed the dashing path of the Black King with his eyes. Ahead of her, the tail of Seiryu high in the air disappeared, leaving a blue afterimage.

The blow, moving so swiftly it couldn't be seen, would knock her feet out from under her, and that was if she managed to avoid it. And even if she did defend against it, the Green King himself would have been hard-pressed to take a blow from this tail unscathed when it was so powerful that it flipped Niko's tank with one hit.

But Kuroyukihime spread out the swords of both arms boldly toward the tail closing in on her, so fast that it couldn't be seen.

Haruyuki gritted his teeth, fully expecting the slender, black-crystal avatar to be blown away like a doll.

Kuroyukihime wrapped both her swords around the tail, almost as if to hug it gently—even though that tail concealed so much power it could have been called the ultimate physical attack.

—Death by Embracing!

Klink! A beam of light flashed, and all sound disappeared from the world. Haruyuki silently watched the slow-motion replay as the giant whip that should have shattered the Black King slipped right through her.

No, that wasn't it...Black Lotus's Terminate Sword had cut Seiryu's lapis lazuli scale-covered tail clean in two, about a meter from the end. This was the insta-kill technique Lotus had once turned on the level-nine Red Rider, the first Red King, to push him to total point loss with a single blow. It was the technique that backed up her nickname of World End.

As the tip of the tail fell to the ground, a blue pillar of water shot up into the sky and scattered.

Here, at last, Seiryu exploded with an angry roar. Writhing in the sky, it dug at the air with the claws on its four limbs. Perhaps in response to the God's quaking rage, the cloudy sky was filled with the rumbling of thunder.

Having succeeded in taking out the tail shock-wave attack, Kuroyukihime whirled around and dashed toward Haruyuki and the others, shouting, "The tail will regenerate soon! We have to get to the other side of the bridge before it does!!"

Haruyuki had already whirled around and started to run by the time her voice reached them. It was still another three hundred meters to the border between the iron of the bridge and the ground's asphalt. In a normal duel, he would have been on the other side before he even knew it, but in this situation, the distance seemed ten times that long.

If Silver Crow flew with two people in his arms and Blood Leopard ran with someone on her back, they could increase the speed of their retreat, but that was a last resort. They had to save Crow's special-attack gauge to deal with Seiryu's most powerful and brutal attack.

Kuroyukihime joined them again soon enough, and the seven ran as a single group once more. The heavyweight-type Cyan Pile was using a technique to accelerate by shooting the pile of his right hand at the ground in order to keep up with them all.

Even without turning around, Haruyuki knew by the sensation of the air around them that the massive angry dragon was hot on their heels in pursuit. Most likely, it would get one more major attack in. If they could make it through that, they'd be able to get to the other side of the bridge.

Now that they didn't have to worry about the tail's shock-wave attack anymore, Takumu would definitely be able to block Thunder Blast. And Utai's Incarnate flames had melted the unknown freezing attack. If Niko summoned her Enhanced Armament again, that should defend them from Water Breath if that was what was coming next. The problem was...

—Our wound shall be healed with your lamentations.
—Sacrifice your many glories to us.

The voice reverberated deeply inside his mind. Holding his breath, Haruyuki looked back over his shoulder and saw it.

Seiryu's front leg was held high, a black sphere growing in the center of the four talons. Semitransparent, the object wobbled and swayed into an irregular shape, like a heavy liquid pushed into a sphere by some minuscule source of gravity. Purple sparks flickered and crawled across the smooth surface.

"Here it comes!!" Kuroyukihime shouted, her voice tense. "Level Drain!!"

Seiryu was finally activating it. Of the God's great many specialized attacks, this one was enormously powerful and perhaps its most brutal. A divine blow that beat down the former level-seven high ranker Aqua Current to level one in a single battle.

Haruyuki took a deep breath and pushed back his fear. "Leave it to me!" he shouted. "You guys keep running!" He spread the silver wings on his back and kicked hard against the bridge surface to take off. As he flipped around to face Seiryu once he had gained a little altitude, he heard voices coming at him from behind:

"Haru, be careful!" Chiyuri cried.

"Don't go flying in the wrong direction!" Niko warned.

He gave a thumbs-up in response and then cleared his mind.

The jet-black sphere was launched with a wet *pop* from the Enemy's talons. The ball flew along slowly at first, but the instant it caught Haruyuki in its sights, it accelerated rapidly and came charging at him.

Haruyuki held his breath and drew it in as close as he dared. Once the 1.5-meter ebony sphere was practically on top of him, he shot upward. With a cumbersome movement, the black sphere curved in the same direction to chase after him.

In the former Nega Nebulus's Castle mission, Aqua Current, the leader of the Seiryu attack squad, stayed alone deep on the bridge to allow her comrades to escape and was hit with this black spherical body any number of times. According to her, the black ball didn't disappear with a direct hit, but instead swallowed the avatar up and began to first eat away at their burst points. Once these were down to zero, it took a level from the Burst Linker, stunning them in the process, and then, finally, the black ball would disappear. That alone was plenty threatening, but what was even more terrifying was that, by the time the level drop came, all the Linker's points had been completely wiped out, so the next time they were hit with the black ball, there would be no grace period; their level would immediately drop down one more.

Put another way, if you could quickly destroy the black ball in the initial point-draining stage, you wouldn't lose a level. But that was a fairly difficult task. The sphere was made out of a highly viscous fluid, and close-range physical attacks were essentially useless. Long-distance attacks, bullets, and lasers all passed through it, and it was quite resistant to fire as well, so there was a strong possibility that the avatar would die before the ball evaporated. Current thought the only tactic that might work was basically to freeze and break the ball.

Unfortunately, none of their current party could use ice

techniques. And dying immediately after getting hit with the black ball would have almost been a better choice, but if they died in the God's territory, there was the risk of not being able to make it out and getting stuck in Unlimited EK. In the end, the best countermeasure was...

"...Shake it off...!" Haruyuki cried in a strained voice. He turned once more, and the end of the bridge came into view. The dark sphere again followed, trailing a tail of sparks.

The orb accelerated without limit when moving in a straight line, so you had to force it to slow down by making it change direction over and over. This was no easy feat above the bridge when it was only thirty meters wide, but if you could also turn up and down and not just left and right—in other words, if you were Silver Crow and had the ability to fly—you might be able to keep running for long enough to get away entirely.

This was the reason Sky Raker had been assigned the role of rescuing Aqua Current, while Haruyuki had stayed with the attack team: to keep his special-attack gauge full and deal with Level Drain.

"Hnn...ngaaah..." He gave his everything to fleeing from the nihilistic lump of liquid, which vibrated unsettlingly as it pursued him. He would fly straight ahead for a few seconds, and then as soon as he sensed the black ball accelerating, turn on a dime. He had trained a fair bit with this zigzag technique during his regular duels with Ash Roller, but the stakes were much higher now. At all costs, he had to avoid turning the wrong way toward Seiryu, or flying out to either side of the bridge. Mustering whatever scrap of spatial awareness there was in his mind and whipping around with dizzying speed, he inched steadily toward the other side of the bridge.

Below him, his comrades were also running full tilt for the border. And although he couldn't see them, Sky Raker—Aqua Current in her arms—would have been on a landing course beyond the black clouds in the sky above. Twenty seconds left until the completion of the mission...

*　　*　　*

—*Small transient ones.*
—*You do well to struggle.*

Haruyuki heard the faint splashing of water, and then a fierce cold wrapped around his entire body. As the world whirled around him, he caught a glimpse of Seiryu launching a second black ball, which quickly began to accelerate in a straight line. And not at Haruyuki. Greedily vibrating, the nihilistic lump charged toward his comrades on the bridge.

"You have to run…!" Haruyuki squeezed out a shout that was more like a shriek as he continued his desperate and random flight.

Running, Kuroyukihime glanced back and saw the black ball closing in. But it was too late. With no twists or turns to navigate, the black ball picked up speed like a bullet shot from a gun and was on the verge of swallowing one of his friends up.

A crimson shadow shot out like lightning—Blood Leopard, who had transformed into Beast mode at some point. The animal avatar fluidly leapt forward from a sharp turn and threw herself at the black sphere. The others stopped in their tracks, radiating shock.

The ball caught Leopard, and the sparks on its surface began to pulsate. Waxing and waning cyclically, it reminded him of the peristalsis of certain blood-drinking creatures— No, it actually *was* sucking, drinking. All the burst points Leopard had accumulated over such a long time. And when it had finished sucking those up, she would be plunged into the nightmare of level drop.

"Pard…!" A cry shot out of Niko. She raced over to Leopard, crouched inside the black ball, and moved to thrust her hand into the sparking liquid. Kuroyukihime stretched a sword hand out to try to stop her, but couldn't reach her. The small, slender fingers were very nearly touching the ebony sphere.

But before they could, Leopard howled, ferociously. The claws of her four paws dug into the iron bridge surface, and the crimson cat pulled away from Niko and began running. The sphere enveloping her body continued to pulsate, so her points had to have been dropping with terrifying speed. Those points could have fallen to zero at any moment, allowing the ball to steal a level and stun her into a motionless state, but the leopard's hard run did not stop. The edge of the bridge was just over a hundred meters away.

Even as he zigzagged above their heads, Haruyuki kept an eye on Leopard racing ahead and the others chasing after her. Staring at the ferocious beast avatar, beautiful even with her torso swallowed up by the black ball, a voice abruptly came back to life in his mind.

—At any rate, it was exactly for this that Pard's sealed away leveling up until today, after all.

Niko had said this in the student council office at Umesato Junior High before the dive into the Unlimited Neutral Field. Blood Leopard was a fairly senior Burst Linker and a soldier who had made a name for herself at the dueling mecca of Akihabara Battle Ground, and she had alluded to having a reason for still being at level six, but Haruyuki hadn't understood what she meant at the time.

"For this"—for the mission to rescue Aqua Current, Leopard had stayed at level six. She had built up a stock of burst points acquired in duels and Enemy hunting without spending them. The years of effort and endurance had all been for this moment. So that even if the black sphere hit her, she could keep running without losing a level. Using her vast cache of points as cushioning, she would have been able to hold on against Seiryu's most brutal attack for a while. All of it was for the moment someday when she would rescue Aqua Current from the God's altar.

In a flash of insight, Haruyuki understood the relationship between Aqua Current, one of the Elements, the senior executive group of the Black Legion, Nega Nebulus; and Blood Leopard, one of the Triplex, the senior executive group of the Red Legion,

Prominence. Although they belonged to different Legions, the two had a similar air about them—they were parent and child.

"...Pard! You can do it...!!" Haruyuki shouted, as he made one sharp turn after another.

Perhaps hearing him, perhaps not, Leopard kicked even more ferociously at the ground and leapt high, high up into the air. At the peak of her trajectory, a faint rainbow rippled outward through the air. Leopard pushed through this, and the ebony sphere that had engulfed her torso broke, scattering into countless droplets. The crimson leopard spun around once in the air before touching down smoothly, the claws of her four paws biting not into dull steel but cracked gray asphalt.

Right behind her, Haruyuki also crossed the dividing line between bridge and earth. And behind *him*, the black sphere smashed into an invisible wall and flew apart. The instant he felt the crisis averted, all the strength drained from his body, and Haruyuki half-fell from the sky. Unable to really stick the landing, his legs crumpled beneath him when he contacted the earth, and he ended up on all fours.

But it was too soon to collapse just yet. Seiryu might come at them with another attack before Kuroyukihime and the others broke free. He tried to stand up, he tried to put strength into his trembling legs when—

"...It's okay" came a quiet voice beside him.

Lifting his head, he saw Blood Leopard. Following the gaze of the entirely graceful and brave animal avatar—even as she was, like him, on all fours on the ground—Haruyuki turned around.

Ardor Maiden, leading the group, was at that moment about to leap off the bridge. Then Lime Bell and Cyan Pile. Lastly, Black Lotus and Scarlet Rain. It seemed that the God Seiryu had abandoned its pursuit when both of its black Level Drain orbs were scattered in all directions.

Still on his hands and knees, Haruyuki looked up at the Super-class Enemy hovering a mere hundred meters away. He could no longer read any emotion in the cold shine of the sapphire eyes. Perhaps because he had left its territory, he also couldn't hear the voice that had echoed in his memory several times. But even so, Haruyuki felt it, the dark, massive, lapis lazuli dragon sneering as if giving them advance notice of their eventual reunion.

Long body undulating, it began to lumber about, changing direction. Its four limbs and their talons, alongside the four pairs of small wings, cut across his vision one after another. Then, the tip of the tail—cut off in Kuroyukihime's Incarnate attack—finally reappeared with soundless regeneration.

The group watched without a word as the massive dragon leisurely flew away and slowly faded out of existence. Finally, the Super-class Enemy, the God Seiryu, vanished as though sucked into the altar five hundred meters away. The watch fires at each corner of the altar then disappeared in turn, and the Century End stage was returned to silence.

—*No.*

He could still hear some kind of sound. A high-pitched resonance, like the howling of the wind, like a reed pipe. Hands once planted on the ground, Haruyuki staggered to his feet and turned his head to the sky. Gradually getting closer, the sound was coming from the other side of the thick layer of black clouds hanging above them.

A few seconds later, a tiny blue light flickered inside the clouds. Glittering like a shooting star, it fell gently down like a bit of fluff. While they held their collective breath and stared up at it, the source of the light finally pushed through the clouds and revealed itself—the flames of boosters, narrowed down to minimum output.

As the light came closer, the figures of the sky-blue avatar with the booster-shaped Enhanced Armament on her back and the light-blue avatar she held in her arms popped up in the night sky. Reflecting back a pale light, the pair descended ever so slowly. A mere five meters or so from the ground, the jet propulsion flames shuddered irregularly and disappeared. The booster's energy gauge was empty.

Haruyuki immediately leapt up and caught the falling avatars in his arms. Before his eyes were two smiling face masks. One of those mouths moved, and a gentle murmur reached his ears:

"Thank you, Corvus."

The other avatar was silent, but the blue eye lenses on the other side of the flowing-water armor blinked softly.

Haruyuki set them down on the ground and took a few steps back to stand alongside Chiyuri and Takumu. A single sentence kept playing over and over and over in his mind:

...*She's back. She's back. She's. Back.*

...For over two and a half years, she had been sealed away on Seiryu's altar. One of the Four Elements, the bouncer who had saved Haruyuki when he was facing total point loss eight months earlier, The One, Aqua Current. In the true sense of the word, she had finally come home to Nega Nebulus—to the Accelerated World.

As he stared, moved to tears, the flowing-water avatar gave them all a meaningful glance before finally facing the crouching crimson leopard a little ways off. Accompanied by the babbling of a brook, she walked over, knelt down, and wrapped both arms around the leopard's neck. She brought her face in close and hugged tightly, so tightly.

"Welcome back, Aki." The fang-filled mouth opened, and Pard offered a brief greeting to her parent.

Current nodded softly. "I'm home, Myah," she replied, as brief as her child. The others watched as the two soundlessly brought their faces together.

After a few seconds, once Current got back to her feet and Leopard returned to human form with the Shape-Change command, Niko slapped her left hand against the fist of her right and shouted, "Allll right! That is mission complete!"

The instant he heard this, the tension in him was suddenly

released, and Haruyuki very nearly slumped to the ground again on weak legs. Someone supported him from behind, and convinced it was Takumu, he leaned back without restraint and let out a long breath.

But it was an unexpected voice that he heard:

"You did well, Crow."

Jumping, he looked back to find the mirrored goggles of the Black King. Flustered, Haruyuki tried to stand up on his own, but Kuroyukihime had turned toward everyone else and begun to talk, so he missed his chance to pull away.

"And all of you, you really did well. You withstood the fierce attacks of the God Seiryu and brought Current back to us. Not to mention that not only did no one else get sealed away, but we didn't see a single death. This is nothing short of a miracle made real by the hard struggle of everyone here. However."

Kuroyukihime stopped for a moment to look at Niko and then Leopard.

"Unfortunately, we did not escape unscathed. First of all, Rain, I apologize for essentially destroying your Enhanced Armament, and I thank you. If we had not had that armor, we would never have been able to make it so deep into the Enemy camp."

"W-well, it was just, you know, you throw me another curry party, and we'll call the whole thing even." The Red King bobbed the antennas on her head as if embarrassed. "Oh! But actually, curry three times in a row, it's, you know…Maybe hamburgers next time? Nah, more Japanese-style, an *okonomiyaki* party."

"…Mm? Hasn't it been two times?"

"What are you talking about? Yesterday—" The Red King abruptly cut herself off, and Haruyuki jumped and stiffened, too.

After the Territories the previous day—June 29—not only had Niko barged into the Arita house and made curry with Haruyuki, but she had stayed over, on top of that. And most likely, the only other person who knew that was Pard.

Kuroyukihime stared suspiciously at the unnaturally silent

Niko and Haruyuki, the latter of which was still frozen in place with her support from behind, but she resumed her speech soon enough. "...Well, I don't care if it's hamburgers or *okonomiyaki* or Buddha Jumps Over the Wall...It'll be after all of this is over."

"R-right, right. Basically, my Enhanced Armament recovers when I dive again, y'know? ...But..." The Red King stopped and turned green eye lenses on her deputy, the person she likely trusted more than anyone else.

Kuroyukihime also looked over at Blood Leopard standing alongside Current and nodded slowly. "...Yes. While there is Rain's loss, we cannot even begin to imagine the damage Blood Leopard took..."

"...What do you mean, Lotus?" Fuko asked, cocking her head to one side. She had been flying through the sky high above, so she hadn't witnessed the scene.

"In the very end, Seiryu attacked with Level Drain." Kuroyuki-hime lowered her eyes and explained in a tense voice. "Just as planned, Crow managed to draw the sphere out of the area for us with his desperate flight, but...I never dreamed it would attack again in quick succession..."

"...! So then, Pard was..."

"Mm. Leopard risked her life to defend us against the second orb. She ran out of the area still in the drain status, and although she managed to avoid a level drop, she must have lost an incredible number of points..."

None of them could say anything to this; they simply stared at Blood Leopard.

"NP." The crimson leopard-person shrugged as though it was seriously no big deal. "Points I saved for this anyway. Can just earn more."

The very first to react was Aqua Current.

"I told you." Akira brought the palm of her hand to Leopard's cheek with a muttered sigh. "You were supposed to forget me."

"Can't forget your parent."

"Stubborn as ever, Myah."

Removing her hand and taking a step back, Akira bowed her head deeply first to Pard and then to Niko. "Thank you, Blood Leopard and the Red King, Scarlet Rain. I will take responsibility for the points Leopard lost in rescuing me and replenish them in full. It might take a little time, but I will absolutely do this."

"I'll help, too." Fuko jumped in before Pard or Niko could react. "Target period of a week, yes?"

"I shall also assist." Utai also raised her right hand without a moment's delay. "I do feel bad for the Enemies, but I'll hunt and hunt and hunt and hunt!"

"In that case, I'll get serious myself. I will give you an ample demonstration of the skill of the hunter they used to call the Genocider in the Shibuya area." When even Kuroyukihime put her name forward like this, the three junior members of Nega Nebulus couldn't stand by in silence.

Takumu, Chiyuri, and Haruyuki all took a step forward together and declared in unison:

"Of course, I'm not that strong, but I'll do what I can!"

"I—I—I mean, it's not much, but I have this search function called Enemy Detector—"

"Detector, schemector. We can just call them with my Acoustic Summon!" Chiyuri cried out forcefully, waving the large bell of her left hand around. "I'll go calling all the Enemies and healing all the dama—" Both voice and movement stopped abruptly, so Haruyuki looked at his childhood friend questioningly.

The yellow-green witch avatar was completely still, as though a time-stopping spell had been cast on her. But an infinity of stars was swirling around, glittering deep in her eye lenses, reminiscent of a cat's eyes. Chiyuri had a surprisingly intellectual side, and this was the sign that the gears in her head were going full speed.

Haruyuki peered at her face, wondering what exactly she had come up with.

"Oh...Ohh! ...Ooooooh!!" Lime Bell suddenly let out a wild cry and whirled her head around, looking at their surroundings.

"Wh-what's going on, Chii?!" a dumbfounded Takumu asked.

No sooner had her eyes locked onto him than Chiyuri was shouting again. "G-gauge! Gimme your special-attack gauge! Right now! Now!!"

"Huh? O-okay, so then smash some ob—"

"There's no time for that! Aah, come on, Haru! Taku! Sit down!!"

Snap! The index finger of her right hand shot out toward the ground, and instantly, Haruyuki and Takumu were seated along-side each other. Standing imposingly before them, Chiyuri brandished the Enhanced Armament of her left hand, Choir Chime, high in the air.

Gong, gong, boooong! With a solemn sound, the bell smacked the heads of the two on the ground from right to left and then back to the right again.

About 20 percent of Haruyuki's health gauge was instantly carried away, and in his field of view, visions of yellow chicks hopped around. Other people's gauges weren't visible in the Unlimited Neutral Field, but Takumu had probably taken about the same amount of damage.

Paying no mind to Kuroyukihime and the others gaping at the sudden violence, Chiyuri glanced up to check her gauge and then shouted again, "Can you go one more time?!"

"Y-y-yeah, I guess," Haruyuki nodded.

"O-of course, Chii!" Takumu puffed his chest out.

Gong, gong, boooong!

The Choir Chime, at first glance a musical instrument, was actually a pretty great weapon. It induced a stun state at the same time as it did damage with a striking attack. After a total of two round trips, and blows to the head on top of that, Takumu and Haruyuki were half-comatose; their upper bodies swayed and wobbled.

Fortunately, Chiyuri's special-attack gauge was apparently full now, and she yanked Choir Chime above her head. "Leopard! Please trust me!!"

She makes a big show of this violence, and then is all "trust me," Haruyuki thought, cradling his head in his hands.

But Pard was nothing if not brave. "'Kay."

"Okay, here we go! Citron—" *Fwm, fwm!* Chiyuri swung the bell of her left hand around twice and then called in a high-pitched voice, "—Caaaaallll!!" She brought Choir Chime down sharply, and a green light gushed forward to swallow Leopard.

Here, finally, Haruyuki—and probably Takumu, too—grasped the intentions of his childhood friend: a recovery measure that was so simple and thus had not occurred to anyone there. Chiyuri was trying to rewind the damage Blood Leopard had taken—not her health gauge, but the burst points Seiryu had stolen.

Lime Bell's special attack, Citron Call, had two modes. Mode I rewound the status of the target avatar in units of time. And Mode II rewound in units of status change. In other words, with Mode I, an emptied health gauge or special-attack gauge could be replenished, while with Mode II, Enhanced Armament summoned by an enemy could be returned to storage. Either ability brought a fearsome advantage in tag team matches and the Territories, earning her the nickname the Watch Witch.

Chiyuri was using Mode I now. But the witch herself had told Haruyuki something once: that neither mode could rewind changes related to level-ups. Meaning, it was impossible to cancel a level promotion and recover the spent points, or cancel a special attack or ability gained as a level-up bonus so that one could make a new selection.

In which case, it seemed to Haruyuki that she wouldn't be able to rewind the burst points stolen by Seiryu. Level increases were saved in the avatar data in the Brain Burst central server at the time they were generated, putting them out of reach of a Burst Linker's individual ability to interfere. It should have been the same for level drops…

—Wait.

That wasn't right. Although Blood Leopard had had her points stolen from her, it hadn't gone so far as a level drop. She hadn't gotten anything in exchange for the deduction of points, so maybe it was possible to rewind that? The points the God Seiryu had sucked up and tucked away in a bag might disappear, but why would they care about that?

"...Chiyu!!" Lost in his thoughts, Haruyuki stood up and supported the shoulders of his childhood friend from behind, as she continued to release light from the bell. "You can do it! You, for sure, I know you can do it!! Keep fighting!!"

Since Citron Call was a special attack and not an Incarnate technique, Haruyuki's encouragement probably wasn't particularly helpful. Even so, he put all the energy he could muster into his hands and tried to support his friend.

Chiyuri had thought and acted on her own before, too, when the twilight marauder, Dusk Taker, had stolen Haruyuki's flight ability, and she eventually got his wings back for him. She was that sort of person. Seemingly willful and selfish, she actually paid more attention than anyone else to the things around her. Most likely, more than half of her motivation for becoming a Burst Linker was for the sake of Haruyuki and Takumu.

...*Thanks, Chiyu.*

A faint silver light grew in the hands of Silver Crow gripping Lime Bell's shoulders, pouring through his armor where they touched. But neither Haruyuki nor Chiyuri—and probably not Kuroyukihime or any of the others, either—noticed this phenomenon.

Before them, wrapped in layers of green light effect, Blood Leopard abruptly stretched her hands toward the sky. Almost as though she were accepting something invisible.

No— Haruyuki could see it, too. White droplets of light pouring down from the night sky. Ephemeral like snowflakes yet somehow warm, the light particles danced down one after another into Leopard's open hands, flashing and disappearing when they touched the armor of her palms.

The strange snow continued to fall for a time and then finally stopped. Chiyuri's special-attack gauge was exhausted.

Lime Bell slowly lowered her Enhanced Armament, and Haru-yuki pulled his hands away from her shoulders and took a step back. But Leopard didn't move right away. As the others held their breath and watched over her, the crimson avatar with the leopard head moved just her left hand, opened her Instruct menu, and flickered around on the page. She quickly found what she was looking for and closed the window, a faint smile linger-ing on the mouth modeled after a ferocious animal.

"Thank you, Lime Bell." Leopard said actual words of appre-ciation and not just her usual "Thanksy" and followed it up with a deep bow. "They're back. The points Seiryu stole, all of them."

After a brief silence, they all erupted in cheers. Niko and Haru-yuki both did double fist pumps, Takumu and Akira bobbed their heads up and down, while Raker and Utai clapped in unison. Amidst all this, Kuroyukihime hovered lightly over to Chiyuri.

"Bell—no, Chiyuri," she murmured, thick with emotion. "I am eternally surprised by you. I thank you. Because of you, we are able to end the mission to rescue Aqua Current in no better way. In the future, too, help me and our comrades with your inven-tiveness and your ability to take action…Thank you."

The sword of her left hand was raised softly, and Chiyuri lightly touched Choir Chime to the flat front of it. "I—I just always charge forward with my hunches," she said, as though embar-rassed. "But I'm really glad I was able to rewind in time. While I was doing it, I thought maybe there was just barely not enough in my special-attack gauge, though."

"…You did?" For some reason, Kuroyukihime glanced at Haru-yuki here, but then quickly returned her gaze to Chiyuri. "No, it's all thanks to your quick-wittedness. I'm truly glad you made it in time…"

"You say that, but aren't you reeeeeally thinking that you're super-lucky to not have to go through the hassle of Enemy hunt-ing?" Niko jeered, putting an end to the tender moment.

"A-and why would I think that?!" Kuroyukihime whirled

around. "Once this entire mission is finished, I couldn't care less if we spent whatever time's left hunting our hearts out!!"

"Oh, now you've said it, Black One! 'Kay then, it's been a while since I took a tour of the four great dungeons—"

""Gah! P-please no!""

Haruyuki and Takumu cried in protest as Niko started laughing in a way that was not clear if she was serious or joking about the whole thing.

"I'll add my own thanks to that pile, Bell." She straightened up again and bowed her head to Chiyuri. "For how you recovered the points for her, but also for how hard you worked for Pard's sake." She patted Chiyuri's arm lightly and took a few steps to face Blood Leopard. "So, Pard? Whatcha wanna do?"

What does she mean, what do you want to do? Haruyuki cocked his head to one side as he watched the red pair with the other black group members.

Pard appeared to think it over for about half a second before nodding slightly. "Go up, right now."

...Go up? Where? Haruyuki cocked his head to the other side, but Pard's left hand was already in motion, opening the Instruct menu. She tapped at the window several times with the tip of her short claw, and after a brief pause, she pressed firmly on some button.

A rainbow circle of light appeared at the avatar's feet, and from it, a similarly rainbow-colored pillar of light rose up to engulf Leopard's entire body. At the same time, a cool and exciting melody played, a sound Haruyuki had heard about four times in the past—the fanfare of a level-up.

"Wh-what?!" he cried out, stunned, and everyone else present, with the exception of Niko, similarly showed varying degrees of surprise.

But Pard's left hand didn't stop there. She brought her index finger up once more and pushed the button again. And so again, the celebration of light and sound swallowed the slender avatar.

"Wh...whaaaaaat?!" His head already thrown back as far as

it could go, Haruyuki was unable to withstand the additional shock and ended up falling backward onto his butt.

Chiyuri to his right and Takumu to his left managed to stay upright, but they were frozen in curious poses. Even Kuroyuki-hime and the senior Linkers lined up across from them simply stood there, speechless.

And it was no wonder. Blood Leopard had, in mere seconds, gone up two levels. Simply going from a level-one newbie to a level three was an immense improvement, but at the moment she'd opened her menu, Pard had been level six. Which meant that she'd gone up one to seven, and then another one—to eight.

Level eight. A true high ranker, with only the Seven Kings of Pure Color being at a higher level. Haruyuki could count on one hand the number of Burst Linkers he knew who had made it that far: only the current deputy of Nega Nebulus, Sky Raker.

In the silence, the rainbow light effect vanished, and Blood Leopard casually let her hand fall back to her side. Since she didn't go through the process of acquiring level-up bonuses or Enhanced Armament, appearance-wise, nothing about her had changed, but Haruyuki definitely felt something like a pressure in the way Pard stood that hadn't been there a minute earlier.

Her long tail swishing, the crimson avatar started to walk soundlessly. She cut past Haruyuki and stopped in front of the sky-blue avatar next to Kuroyukihime. Bloody Kitty, aka Blood Leopard, faced the Nega Nebulus deputy Strato-Shooter, aka Sky Raker, and said briefly in a quiet voice, "Sorry for the wait, Raker."

"You finally made it this far, hmm, Leopard?" Fuko responded with similar brevity.

Haruyuki intuitively understood the meaning of this exchange. He'd heard that Leopard and Raker were rivals, and they had fought any number of fierce battles in the Territories and normal duels. Pard had no doubt made incredible efforts to level up in lockstep with Fuko. But in the summer three years earlier, the former Nega Nebulus had been destroyed, and their duels had ended. Leopard had stopped leveling up in order to rescue Aqua Current sealed away at the Castle, and Raker had determined that the responsibility for the destruction of the Legion was her fault and thus retired from duels.

And then today, two years and ten months after the Castle Fight. Aqua Current had been rescued, and Blood Leopard had used the points she'd been saving that whole time to become level eight—to reach the same height as Sky Raker. *That* was what their exchange meant.

As they faced each other, their bodies were wrapped in a hazy overlay. It wasn't that they were trying to activate any Incarnate technique; it was simply that the fighting spirit and delight building inside their avatars had become an aura and leaked out. The pair simultaneously raised their right hands and clenched them into fists—and then slowly touched them to each other. The concentrated auras bounced off each other, sparking sky-blue and crimson.

Naturally, not now, but at some point in the near future, the two would fight. The techniques they'd polished and perfected, the experience they'd accumulated, their pride as Burst Linkers, they would put all of it into their fists and tell each other so, so much. Haruyuki didn't know whether he'd get to watch that fight or not, but even if he couldn't, he was certain of just one thing: After the fight, the bond between the two would be that much deeper, and only stronger.

Taking his gaze off the two level eights, Haruyuki unconsciously looked over at Cyan Pile standing next to him. Takumu happened to turn his face at the same time, and their gazes intersected for a moment.

Even if he couldn't put it into words, his childhood friend's thoughts came across loud and clear. He was remembering again the promise to duel that they had confirmed with each other while they were moving on the armored truck from Suginami to the Castle. Once they were both level seven, they would duel for real, with the fullest extent of their abilities. Whatever they gained or lost as a result—

"...!" Surprised by his own thoughts, Haruyuki opened his eyes wide beneath his mirrored mask. If Silver Crow's goggles hadn't been half-mirrored, he would have been getting some raised eyebrows from Takumu, but fortunately, his childhood friend appeared to have noticed nothing. He nodded and then turned his face forward again, but his mind was locked as it had been a few seconds before.

...Lose? When Takumu and I duel, whoever wins or loses, we won't actually lose anything. The way we've been...I'm sure it's the way we'll be, Haruyuki told himself, brushing away the baseless premonition.

Fuko and Pard lowered their fists at basically the same time. The crimson, humanoid leopard whirled around and returned to her place, just behind Niko's right.

The Burst Linkers, now numbering nine since they'd welcomed one more person, rearranged themselves spontaneously into a large circle.

Their commander, Kuroyukihime, nodded briefly and raised the sword of her right arm. "Mission number one, Operation Aqua Current Rescue, is now complete," she announced firmly. "You all performed wonderfully. In conclusion, once again, welcome back, Curren."

"Welcome back!!" Niko and Pard also sang out.

"...I'm home, everyone," Akira said, enunciating each syllable, slowly blinking eye lenses beneath the flowing water that covered her face mask.

Haruyuki had to have been seeing things to imagine that even through the film of water, Akira's eyes looked warm and damp.

3

The post-mission processing—recovering everyone's health gauges and refreshing Niko's Enhanced Armament, which had been pounded full of holes under Seiryu's fierce attacks—required roughly an hour.

The means for it was incredibly simple. They returned to the real world briefly through a leave point in Tokyo Station and then immediately reaccelerated. Although this used up an additional ten points, their duel avatars and the Enhanced Armament were completely regenerated. It felt like mere seconds in experienced time for Haruyuki and his friends, but while they were shouting the Unlimited Burst command, about a thousand times that much time passed in the Accelerated World.

Compared to the many online games Haruyuki had played before Brain Burst, the complete recovery of health and equipment with just one re-log-in seemed fairly generous, but there was a problem: When you used a portal, your location information was also reset.

Thus, when Haruyuki touched down in the Accelerated World once more, the scene around him was not Tokyo Station. Instead, he had returned to the yard of Umesato Junior High. And on top of that, in the mere hour they had been away, the Change had apparently come, so that the night of the Century End stage had lifted, and the grounds were dyed red, as though they were on fire.

He had been so impatient to get back, he had shouted the command at the fastest speed the BB program recognized, so no one else had dived in with him yet. And since a difference of 0.1 seconds bloated up into a hundred seconds on this side, it would take a minute or more for his companions to join him.

Haruyuki turned around and looked at the Umesato Junior High school buildings, transformed now into something resembling Grecian temple ruins. He narrowed his eyes to stare at one corner on the east side of the first floor of the second school building.

In the nurse's room that existed in that spot in the real world, right now at that very moment, his cherished friend, Rin Kusakabe, was fighting with everything she had. She was desperately trying to endure the mental interference of the ISS kit parasitizing the American motorcycle that was a part of her duel avatar, Ash Roller.

Rin had collapsed in the middle of the school festival right after watching the boys' kendo team group performance, so in real-world time, thirty minutes had not yet passed. But since the power of an individual ISS kit's interference grew in step with the spread of the infection through the Accelerated World, one minute must have felt any number of times longer than that to Rin, who was struggling to keep the kit from taking control.

They had learned that you couldn't get away from the kit's interference even if you removed your Neurolinker or switched the power off from when Takumu had been parasitized. Haruyuki had no idea what the logic behind it was, but as long as the ISS kit existed inside the Neurolinker—or as long as the kit's main body existed inside the Brain Burst central server—the phenomenon would continue.

"...Kusakabe. Hang on just a little longer." Haruyuki started talking to Rin in the real world. "Curren's back, and Pard's level eight now. We're all going right now to take out Metatron and destroy the ISS kit main body. And then let's go check out the rest of the festival together. There's still a bunch of stuff I want to show you. And your brother— Ash, I want to properly introduce him to everyone. So…So…"

He fumbled earnestly to string these words together, but the fretful feeling in his heart didn't go away. It was as though all the things he had pushed back so he could concentrate on the mission to rescue Aqua Current were now forcing their way up and out of him.

What if they failed to destroy the kit main body?

The only means left, then, to stop the mental interference for Rin would be for her to stop being a Burst Linker—for Ash Roller to be erased. Ash had been Haruyuki's first fight, his first loss, his first win in the Accelerated World, and he was just as important to Haruyuki now as any of his Legion companions. And he felt the same about Rin, who had worked hard to pull Haruyuki back when he was on the verge of pushing for total point loss so he could take the Armor of Catastrophe out with him. Both were priceless, invaluable friends to him.

They couldn't fail. Failure was not an option. If success or failure in the Metatron mission rested on Haruyuki's Optical Conduction ability, then even if it meant sacrificing himself, he would repel the laser attack that was powerful enough to rend the earth asunder.

He clenched his hands into tight fists as he stared at the corner of the second school building, and the sound of an avatar appearing came from behind him. He turned to find Lime Bell—Chiyuri—flying down inside a circle of light. She had no sooner set eyes on him than she was exploding into one of the lectures she was so adept at.

"I get that you're in a hurry, Haru, but your command was too fast! What if you'd gotten pushed back?! You'd end up making all of us wait however many minutes instead!"

Haruyuki mentally sent a few last words of encouragement toward Rin in the real world before arguing with some force,

"Wh-whatever! The BB command and my special-attack names are the only things I never stammer over!"

"I wonder about that…"

When she stared at him with those doubtful eyes, he felt like maybe he had once or so, and he tried to force the conversation onto a different track.

"A-anyway, dawn came with the Change. And when I see the morning light, I get reflexively sleepy, you know?" He made like he was yawning.

But Chiyuri only narrowed her eyes further and glared. "So in the world you're in, the sun rises in the west?" she retorted.

"Huh?" He hurriedly shook his head from side to side. The red sun was indeed hanging just above the horizon not in the direction of Shinjuku, but rather Mitaka. The orange of the sky that Haruyuki had been convinced was the sunrise was actually sunset. But to meekly admit his mistake here would be a loss of face as the senior Burst Linker. "W-we don't know whether that's the real sun or not! It could just be a huge ball of flames burning in Hachioji."

Chiyuri's eyes became even cooler at this cringeworthy counterargument, digging into Haruyuki from above. "If something like that was over there burning, the Burst Linkers who dived in the Hachioji area would be killed instantly. And this is a Twilight stage. Twilight means when the sun is setting, so if that's not the evening sun, then what is it?"

"…Y-you have a point…" Effortlessly backed into a corner, Haruyuki twisted the index fingers of both hands together to indicate his obvious submission.

"Heh-heh!" He heard the laughter-filled voice of Kuroyukihime, who had appeared behind them at some point. "I also believe that is the sun, but I can't say with utmost certainty that Haruyuki's assertion is mere tall tales either."

"Huh? What do you mean, Kuroyukihime?"

Just as Haruyuki turned around, the rest of his comrades

appeared, one after another. After a glance to check that all nine members were present, the Black King adroitly crossed her sword arms.

"In the Unlimited Neutral Field, verrrrrry occasionally, the Legend-class Enemy Sun God Inti appears. The only way to describe it, I suppose, is that it's a massive ball of flames that rolls around on the ground. It absorbs fire-type attacks, evaporates water-type attacks, and on top of that, if you get near it, you die instantly from high-temperature damage. I doubt there has ever been a Legion that's defeated Inti."

"I-I'd like to never run into it."

"I wanna see it!"

When Haruyuki and Chiyuri expressed totally opposing opinions, Akira stepped forward, accompanied by the sound of flowing water. "A long time ago, just once, I fought Inti," she said nonchalantly.

"R-really, Curren? I've only ever seen it from afar."

"Graph and I found it when we were out hunting Enemies. I tried to run away, but that idi—reckless one said he had a good strategy..."

The "idi—reckless one" Akira was referring to was the last of Nega Nebulus's Four Elements, Graphite Edge. He led the squad attacking the north gate in the Castle attack mission and fought the God Genbu before ending up in the same Unlimited EK state as Utai and Akira. That was basically all Haruyuki knew about him, but apparently, he was the sort of avatar who was always raring for a fight.

Complicated looks rose upon the face masks of Fuko and Utai, who had joined the circle of conversation at some point, while Niko grinned and Pard looked exasperated.

Akira glanced at them all and then continued the ballad of the ancient adventure. "Graph's plan was to pull Inti to somewhere with a large amount of water, knock it in there, and extinguish the flames. We were in Aoyama, so we drew it all the way to the

Akasaka imperial garden two kilometers away, death breathing down our necks the whole time. And somehow, we managed to get it to fall into the pond."

"...S-so then, did Inti's flames go out...?" Takumu asked with excited interest from behind Haruyuki.

Akira shrugged slightly. "The flames weakened for just a moment, but the pond—which is two hundred meters around—was boiling in a flash, and Graph got incinerated attacking it with a sword, so I left it and ran. When he regenerated, that idi—that boy who easily gets carried away, said he was going to keep it chasing him around the city until the stage changed to a Storm. And then he was going to drop it into Tokyo Bay for good measure."

"Ha-ha-ha-ha!" Here, Niko erupted in laughter as though she could no longer hold it in. "Just like Negabu's Anomaly! I've heard all kinds of rumors, and it sounds like he was seriously quite the mighty hero."

"For him, you have to add *idiot* before *hero*, Red King." Fuko smoothly uttered the adjective that Akira had hesitated to, leaned back in her wheelchair, and looked up at the madder-red sky. After a brief pause, sounding somehow concerned, she said, "Speaking of the Change...I didn't expect we would be so lucky as to get a Hell stage, but I can't really say a Twilight stage is such a good omen."

"Huh...?" *Why is that, Master?* Haruyuki was about to ask, but a moment sooner, Takumu naturally slipped into professor mode.

"Right. The Archangel Metatron's power is weaker in a dark-type stage. So then a holy-type stage—albeit a low-level one like Twilight—would add a positive correction to Metatron's status, right?"

"Just a little, but yes. Still, it's a fact that in a battle of extremes, that 'little' might influence the state of the game...Lotus, I leave the decision to you."

"Mm..." The leader of this mission, Kuroyukihime, looked up at the dusky sky, as Fuko had. "When we went back to the other side for just a moment, the time was 12:20:15. In other words, we have nine minutes and forty-five seconds left until the forced disconnect safety set for twelve thirty is activated...We have 585,000 seconds on this side, which equals 162.5 hours, which equals six days and eighteen hours and thirty minutes."

Being able to churn out conversions between Accelerated World and real-world time like that is another mark of a high ranker, huh? Haruyuki thought in one corner of his mind as he concentrated on Kuroyukihime's voice.

"During that time, there will be at least one change, and if we're lucky, two. The battle against Metatron will likely—no, definitely—be a short one, so it would in theory be possible to wait for the next Change somewhere safe. Of course, there is a nonzero chance that the next stage will be a higher-level holy type, but in my experience, holy and dark types essentially never appear twice in a row. If we're going to play it safe, we'll go on standby for three days—"

"K-Kuroyukihime!" Haruyuki shouted, unconsciously stepping forward. "It's okay. No matter what the stage is, I'll make sure to definitely repel Metatron's laser! So no standby or anything, right away—" He frantically flapped his lips, a picture of Rin on a bed in the nurse's room in the back of his mind the whole time.

Even supposing they did spend three days on the inside, only four minutes and a bit would pass on the outside. But right now, Haruyuki couldn't see that time as "only." They had to free Rin from her suffering even one minute, one second faster. This was the promise Haruyuki had made when he took on the challenge of the two major missions back-to-back.

"...Right now, we have to go to Midtown Tower!" Haruyuki pushed each word brokenly from his trembling chest and clenched his right hand into a tight fist.

A hand covered in a cool film of water gently wrapped around that fist. The endlessly flowing water gently eased Haruyuki's fitful impatience. "I completely understand how you feel, Crow."

The owner of the voice was Aqua Current, recently freed from a sealed state. Moving to stand in front of him, she stared hard at Haruyuki with eyes pale like the light of the moon reflected on the surface of water.

"A very long time ago, back when I still hadn't joined the Legion, I wasn't able to help someone very important to me. This was someone very strong with incredibly big dreams, but...people were jealous and feared her, and their malice swallowed her up. Which is why I really do understand your wanting to hurry and save Ash Roller without wasting a single second. But that's all the more reason why we can't rush this. It's not that anyone doubts your abilities. But you can't win against Metatron by yourself. For all of us to give it everything we've got, we need to collect as much information as there is to collect, discuss it all again and again and again, and prepare as thoroughly as we can. That's what's needed right now." For Akira, this was a very long and very emotional speech.

Haruyuki slowly relaxed his shoulders and hung his head deeply. "...But...Three days—I mean, wait for three days...During that time, Kusakabe's..."

"I'm not saying three days. But will you give us a day—no, one night?"

Off to the left of Haruyuki's hanging head, he heard a powerful voice, as if shaking off its hesitation. He lifted his eyes and looked into the face of the swordmaster, Kuroyukihime. Beneath her inky goggles, her violet-blue eyes shone resolutely.

"We won't rely on the Change. Our attacks won't hit Metatron in anything other than a Hell stage anyway. There's nothing to be done about slight status corrections. But we do need to scout the area around Midtown Tower and reexamine the details of our strategy. And...I'm sure no one is aware of it right now, but the exhaustion from the battle with Seiryu before is still with us. We'll rest a night, recover our mental energy, and take on Metatron in top condition. So that we can definitely save your friend—Ash Roller."

"...Okay!" Haruyuki took a deep breath and nodded forcefully. Prompt action and a reckless charge were totally different things. Up to that point, he had any number of times thoughtlessly barged into all kinds of situations and made everyone worry, but if he really wanted to make it to level seven—to become a high ranker—then it was about time he learned the importance of knowledge and thought. But also, so he didn't disappoint Takumu in their promised duel.

...Kusakabe, just twelve more hours. Hang on for just forty-three seconds in the real world. And then we'll end all of this.

He sent this third thought to Rin and then switched mental gears to the business of strategy. First, a night of rest. That said, there were a limited number of places where they could rest safely in the Unlimited Neutral Field, given the Enemies swarming around, and all the more so in a Twilight stage with all the buildings now half-destroyed like Greek ruins.

"Um, so then, first of all, where...?" Haruyuki turned to look at Kuroyukihime, Akira, and the veteran squad, but everyone was wrestling with the same question. He didn't get an answer right away.

"Um, is it a big no to resting in the school?" Chiyuri asked. "Although, I guess the walls and floors are all busted up, but..."

"Well, it's not that we can't rest here," Niko replied. "But we'd hafta post a sentry so we don't get attacked by Enemies or other Burst Linkers. That's kind of a hassle, y'know? You don't even have anyone to talk to or anything."

"Hee-hee-hee, it's okay, Niko, sweetie! I'll keep watch with you so you don't get lonely!" Chiyuri teased.

"Wh-who said anything about lonely?! And quit it with the 'sweetie' crap!"

Watching this with a smile, Utai looked back as though she had suddenly remembered something. "Speaking of places to rest, Fu, can we not rest *there*?" she asked.

"Mm-hmm, I thought of that, too, but it's a little far," Fuko replied. "From the east gate of the Castle, it's just a little to the south, though. That would've been nice."

...*There? Far? South of the east gate?* Haruyuki input all this data into the computer in his mind, and the answer popped out with a *ding!*

"Oh, right!" he shouted. "Master Raker has a house, doesn't she?! No Enemies or Burst Linkers can get in there, so we could sleep in peace—" Here, he remembered exactly what he had been through at that house, and his mouth snapped shut.

Haruyuki had visited Sky Raker's player home, a house built on top of the old Tokyo Tower, two and a half months earlier. He had begged her to teach him the Incarnate System, and smiling gently, Raker had stretched out her right hand and mercilessly pushed him off—to the ground far, far below from a height of three hundred thirty-three meters.

No way, that wouldn't happen again—no, no, no way. I mean, I've already mastered Incarnate techniques, and I have my wings back, too. Even as he told himself this, Haruyuki was seized by an ominous premonition, even while the discussion proceeded among the girls.

"Mm, I see. Yes, Fufuan. It *is* a little far from here, but fortunately, we have been allocated a taxi."

"Now, look here, I'm gonna start charging you! And where exactly is this *Foo-foo-an* anyway—Shiba Park?! Deep in Oscillatory, with Aurora just off to the right?! That's haunted territory! Why would you—?"

"Hee-hee, it's the highest player home in all twenty-three wards of Tokyo, Red King. Currently, the only ones who can make it up there on their own are me and Corvus, and...Ash on a good day."

Although a pained look flickered across her face when she spoke Ash Roller's name, Fuko quickly regained her smile and continued.

"If we go the way we went before and then straight south from Kasumigaseki in the Chiyoda area, we can basically make it without really passing through Oscillatory Universe territory. But we used a lot of Incarnate techniques in the battle with Seiryu, so Beast-class Enemies might be gathering in that area right about now. It's a little bit longer, but it would probably be better if we went up Yamate Street to Shinagawa and then go north."

"But then we're cuttin' right through GW territory? Those guys love Enemy hunting. We might run into a huge party. It *is* Sunday afternoon and all."

"Mm. Well, we'll manage somehow."

"You can't seriously be planning to chop them all down and pass through, yeah? I'm totally not into giving ol' Iron Fists a reason to whine and complain at the next meeting of the Seven Kings. That guy's such a pain in the butt."

"Goodness, Fists can be quite adorable, though, you know. When I caught his rocket punch in midair and we all tickled it and pinched it and did all sorts of things, his reaction really made me burst out laughing."

"...You seriously get around and do your thing, Strong Arm," Niko said, her red face mask paling slightly, and Pard bobbed her head up and down in her usual position behind the king.

Kuroyukihime cleared her throat and brought the derailed conversation back on track. "A-anyway, I think the Shinagawa course from Shibuya is relatively less dangerous," she said, sounding more like she was posing a question to all present. "The real headquarters for Oscillatory is hypothesized to be a girls' school that goes all the way from elementary through university in Shirokane, Minato Ward, but there won't be any problems if we move at a distance of more than two kilometers from there. Anyone have any opinions?"

Chiyuri's right hand twitched, but she stayed silent beside him. Haruyuki could basically guess what his childhood friend was thinking at that moment. She'd probably been about to ask Kuroyukihime why she had such detailed real info on the White Legion, which had its territory in distant Minato Ward.

Given that the majority of Burst Linkers were elementary,

junior high, or high school students, it was often the case that key Legion bases were the schools attended by the master or the senior executive. Nega Nebulus itself was like that, and the small Legion Petit Paquet they had encountered in the Setagaya area was the same.

Thus, there was a certain level of risk at play if the name of the school/Legion base got around, although perhaps not on the level of an individual Burst Linker being cracked in the real. Kuroyukihime used her privileges as student council vice president to set up various defensive measures against any leaks, and Oscillatory Universe had to have been doing the same. Identifying the headquarters from outside was difficult in the extreme.

But of course, this information hadn't been obtained from the outside. The Black King was the in-game scion and actual younger sister of the White King, White Cosmos. The reason Kuroyukihime knew the White Legion's base was because she was a relative who had once lived with her under the same roof.

Kuroyukihime herself had informed Haruyuki of this after school three days earlier in the student council office of Umesato Junior High. The only other people there who likely knew were the three Elements, but given how sharp her natural intuition was, Chiyuri had probably figured out that there was some kind of relationship between Kuroyukihime and the White King. Haruyuki was sure Kuroyukihime would talk to her and Takumu in the not-so-distant future about everything, about the series of events leading up to her split from her "parent," the White King.

Whether she was aware of Haruyuki's thoughts or not, Kuroyukihime nodded slowly and brought the discussion to a close. "Now, at any rate, we appear to have no opposing opinions, so we'll all fill our special-attack gauges, just in case, and then head first toward the old Tokyo Tower on a southward course. If the Red King aaaaaaabsolutely insists she does not want to drive, we will have no choice but to walk the twenty kilometers."

"Ugh! Honestly! Fine, I get it!" Niko cried, waving her right hand around. But then, with a grin, she countered, "But sneaking around on these back roads is a total hassle. We're taking the main streets! We run into any big Enemies and I'm charging right through 'em. You fall off, you get back up on the roof on your own!"

Despite this wild call, Niko's driving was actually quite restrained, compared with their earlier trip. The armored truck, like new after being refreshed in the second dive, rolled down Oume Highway at a speed of forty kilometers per hour and took a right at Nakano-sakaue Station. Once they got onto Yamate Street, the sixth of the eight roads encircling the city center, she sped up only slightly.

Just as the Shinjuku Government Building rising up to their immediate left indicated, this area was smack in the middle of Blue Legion territory, but fortunately, there was no sign of any Enemy hunting parties. To start with, even if they set up a long-term camp for a continuous month, that was only about forty-five minutes in the real world. Unexpected encounters with other Burst Linkers were relatively rare.

If there were no hunts going on, then it stood to reason that the possibility of encountering an Enemy would increase, but even when they passed through the center of Shinjuku, Yamate Street was blanketed in silence. The Twilight stage wasn't the best for their current mission, but the excellent visibility that came from all the buildings transformed into ruins was a blessing.

Kuroyukihime, Akira, Utai, Pard, and Chiyuri were merrily chatting away in the center of the roof, but having volunteered to keep watch, Haruyuki alone was sitting at the very front of the vehicle with watchful eyes. They passed through Shinjuku, and a large grassy field came into view up ahead on the left. The temple standing alone in the center with little in the way of ruins damage had to have been Meiji Shrine. Which meant that on the other side was the Shibuya area.

"Corvus, it seems like you don't often go to Shibuya. Is there a reason for that, I wonder?" The question came abruptly from behind him.

Haruyuki jumped and looked over his shoulder. His eyes landed on Fuko's gentle smile as she sat in her wheelchair, having taken his back at some point. "Um, oh, nothing in particular. It's not like that, but..." Shrinking into himself, he mumbled, "It's like, Shibuya and Harajuku, I mean, there's this image, like you go buy clothes and stuff there or, um, like you go on d-dates...I guess I just never...had the need to go, you know..."

Fuko blinked and then smiled broadly. "I'm sorry. I wasn't clear. I mean to ask why you don't go duel there."

"Heh..."

He felt like Niko in the cockpit below was holding in a laugh, but Haruyuki didn't have the mental wiggle room to respond to that. He waved his hands wildly in front of his face.

"R-right! Please forget what I said! Um, the reason I don't duel in the Shibuya area...B-basically, I don't really go there in the real, so I don't know the lay of the land too well. And I kinda figured that if I rubbed the Green Legion, GW, the wrong way and they came at us for real in the Territories, we'd be in trouble."

"You needn't worry about that second reason. GW's Six Armors aren't the type of people to get revenge for normal duels in the Territories. Probably...But the only thing to be done about your first reason is resolve it with experience."

"E-experience...What do you...?"

"Once this mission is over, I'll show you around Shibuya. There are a lot of shops I could show you that I think you'd like, Corvus?"

"Sh-shops? Not like...an Accelerated World shop, but..."

"Real-world arcades, used bookstores, things like that. Of course, I don't care at all if you'd prefer to go buy 'clothes and things.'"

"Th—"

That's basically a da— The moment this flashed through his mind, he heard a voice from below once more, and it didn't come via the speaker.

"Hey, gimme a break already. Don't go making dates right on top of someone's head here!"

"D—" He was about to shout, *It's not a date—it's training!* when it suddenly occurred to him. Naturally, he wasn't averse to being alone with Fuko, but if they were going to take a field trip to Shibuya, a big group would definitely be more fun.

He took a deep breath before somehow regaining his calm and turning around. "I understand, Master. So on our next free day, we'll all go to Shibuya. With Niko and Pard and Kuroyukihime and Takumu and everyone…And of course, Rin, too."

"Yes, let's do that." Fuko kindly narrowed her madder-red eye lenses and nodded slowly twice. "Those green kids will get quite the surprise, hmm?"

"H-hey! I wasn't saying you gotta drag me along or something, you know!" Niko shouted as if flustered, then added, "I'm not saying I won't go, though."

Haruyuki and Fuko laughed out loud together.

Even after they passed through Shibuya and entered Meguro, the road was quiet. Engine gently rumbling, the armored vehicle moved forward along the dusky main highway, ruined temples lining both sides. Ebisu, Meguro, Gotanda—Haruyuki had absolutely no opportunity to visit the south side of the city center in either the real or Accelerated World, so he gradually lost track of where they were at any given moment. The massive setting sun off to the right had shifted at some point to directly behind them, and with that, he finally realized that their direction had changed from south to east.

Great Wall, which controlled the three areas of Shibuya, Meguro, and Shinagawa, was without a doubt the largest organization in the Accelerated World in terms of both territory size and number of members. But their policies were the most moderate of the six Legions that had signed the mutual nonaggression pact, and they very rarely went on group trips to even the neutral areas. Although they sent an attack team to Nega Nebulus's territory during the Territories every weekend, the group was usually made up of level twos and threes, up to five at the highest—which gave Haruyuki the impression that GW was trying to give their younger members experience rather than take Negabu's territory.

The Green Legion poured the majority of their strength into hunting large Enemies in the Unlimited Neutral Field. Accordingly, the Green King, Green Grandé, was powerful enough to be able to safely hunt Wild-class solo, and he earned a massive quantity of burst points on his frequent long-term hunting trips.

What was different about Grandé was that he turned all those hard-won points into card items and then fed them to the weakest Lesser-class Enemies. And he didn't limit this feeding to Shibuya and Meguro, so parties from other Legions could also hunt these so-called bonus Enemies to win large numbers of points. This was actually more often the case than not.

In other words, the Green King was redistributing the points obtained from Enemies around the Unlimited Neutral Field, with the point of this work being the continuation and expansion of the Accelerated World, of the fighting game Brain Burst 2039. When Haruyuki met him by chance on the roof of the Roppongi Hills Tower, Grandé explained his reasons using unfamiliar terms.

Trial number one aka Accel Assault 2038.

Trial number three aka Cosmos Corrupt 2040.

They had both been abandoned due to the exit of all the players. But Brain Burst 2039, trial number two, was equipped with some elements that the other two did not have. Until it became clear what these were, the world could not be permitted to be closed.

While all of this was utterly incomprehensible to Haruyuki, it was also terrifying at the same time. Especially the word *trial*. If it was the *trial* of "a series of trials and errors," then didn't that mean this world that had saved Haruyuki, guided him, and given him so much was nothing more than a fleeting fiction to be extinguished on a whim? So Haruyuki had so far not taken the time to think too deeply about the Green King's words.

It wasn't that he blindly feared the destruction of the Accelerated World. As long as the master of swords, Kuroyukihime, the person he loved and respected more than anyone, achieved her dream of reaching level ten and as a result, cleared the game, he thought he might like to watch the end of the world by her side. He felt like, in that case, he would be able to get something just as big and important, even if the Accelerated World vanished.

But the idea of some unknown entity deciding it was a failure and flicking a switch to make everything disappear—all of it reduced to zero with them only halfway through, taking along for the ride the memories of each and every Burst Linker—he absolutely hated this possibility. But at the same time, he was at a level where he could do nothing about it on his own, something that was so frightening it made him tremble.

On the verge of actually shaking, Haruyuki pinned his avatar down with both hands and switched mental gears. Right now was not the time for thinking about things outside the world that he'd never be able to touch; he need to focus on the precious friends who were, at that very moment, suffering nearby. Rin Kusakabe and Ash Roller had helped Haruyuki any number of times, so this time, he would help them.

Lifting his face, he spotted a double-arched bridge up ahead, like the aqueducts of Roman times. He peered at it and wondered what it could have been in the real world when Fuko, who had been behind him the whole time, began to explain.

"I suppose that would be the Yamanote Line bridge and the Shinkansen bridge? Once we go through that and make a left onto Dai-ichi Keihin, Shinagawa Station is basically right there. And then we ride another four or five kilometers north, and we're at the old Tokyo Tower."

The tank went exactly the way Fuko said, and in a few minutes, the chalky tower piercing the distant sky came into view. Reflecting the eternal twilight, the tower was dyed red on the left side and purple on the right. His friends chatting in the rear also moved to the front of the vehicle.

"Ah, it's so pretty!" Chiyuri let out a cry of wonder on the party's behalf. "I've never seen the old Tokyo Tower in a Twilight stage before!"

"Now that you mention it, neither have I," Haruyuki said, unconsciously competitive.

"Of course it's my first time," Takumu chimed in. "It's already been ninety years since the real thing was built, and it has a grandeur that really makes you feel that, huh?"

Aaah, Taku, you always know the right thing to say! Haruyuki thought admiringly.

"Just like Four Eyes to say something professor-y!" Niko's voice rang out from the speaker.

At the moment the red armored trailer rode into Shiba Park east of Minato Ward area—it had become customary to remove the term *Ward* for all twenty-three Tokyo segments besides Kita Ward and Minato Ward—precisely thirty minutes had passed since the start of their second dive.

A mere three kilometers north was the east gate of the Castle where their fierce battle with the God Seiryu had unfolded. The thought did cross his mind that it would have been nice if they could have saved their position when they left through the portal, but Brain Burst—in principle, a fighting game—could not be expected to have a such a useful feature as that.

When the passengers had climbed down from the roof and Niko had returned the Enhanced Armament to storage and landed on the ground, the nine Burst Linkers stood in a row and gazed up at the massive tower, twenty meters or so in diameter.

In the real world, the old Tokyo Tower was a tapering radio tower made of linked steel, but in the Accelerated World, it appeared as a pillar with the same surface area at the top and bottom. Naturally, the wall was perfectly perpendicular all around, and there was no ladder or elevator.

When Haruyuki had tried to climb it with his bare hands for his Incarnate training two and a half months earlier, it had been a Wasteland stage and all the buildings had turned into rocky mountains, so the wall before him had been suitably sturdy. But now it was made of smooth marble, with basically no indentations that could act as foot- or handholds. The buildings of the Twilight stage were brittle, so they could probably poke holes in the wall, but...

"...Master, I'll ask just in case: What would happen if you made a bunch of holes in this tower...?"

"It would break, of course." Fuko grinned. "It would be restored in the next Change, but I don't think I'd ever forget the fact that you destroyed my house, Corvus."

"I—I won't break it! No way!" Haruyuki flinched into himself.

"Whoa, Fuko," Kuroyukihime interjected with a wry laugh. "Don't threaten my child unduly. Large geographical features in the Unlimited Neutral Field don't break as easily as all that."

"Hee-hee-hee, I suppose that's so. But I'm a little interested in seeing whether my house would simply float in the air if the tower did break, or if it would come crashing down to the ground."

"Hmm. Given that normally, coordinates are fixed, I suppose it would...float..."

"Oh! If we're experimenting, I can knock the tower away with my big guns!" The dangerous proposal had no sooner been made than Niko was moving to actually re-summon her Enhanced Armament.

Pard scooped her up in her arms and silently shook her head.

"H-hey, Pard! Don't treat me like a kid! I wasn't really gonna do it or anything!"

"...Your voice was dead serious."

"...It was."

Akira and Utai commented with straight faces while Chiyuri

and Takumu burst out laughing. They all giggled together for a minute before Haruyuki returned to the original conversation.

"Um, so then, just in case, it seems like we should give up on the idea of punching holes in it and climbing up. Which means our only choice is for Master and me to carry everyone, but all at once…is prob'ly not going to work."

The height of the tower was near the maximum altitude of Gale Thruster, so Fuko would only be able to fly there with one person. And no matter how Haruyuki looked at it, there was no way he could yank up the remaining six all in one go.

"You can just take us there in two groups. Sorry, but—," Kuroyukihime started to say.

"I can probs climb it," Pard announced, Niko still tucked under her left arm, as she touched the marble surface with a hand.

"What?! Leopard, do you happen to have the ability to run up walls?"

"I took my level-up bonus while we were moving," the leopard-headed avatar informed them smoothly.

They all eyed her doubtfully for a moment before crying out in unison—with one exception—"Whooaaa!"

"B-but Pard, we're not talking a level-two or -three bonus here! This is seven and eight! Which means they're basically your last ones. When you're choosing something like that, you have to spend a week or two weeks or a month or six months just thinking it over," Haruyuki rattled on without pause.

"NP." Pard shrugged lightly and said something astounding. "You make a mistake, it's not like there's no recovery method."

The slight breeze of the Twilight stage gusted up and when it died back down, they—except for one—cried out again in surprise.

""""Whaaaaat?!"""""

"I-is that true, Leopard?!" Kuroyukihime pressed in close. "Even *I've* never heard talk of that!"

"Seriously, Pard?! You know something like that, you need to be telling me first!" Niko wailed, still being held by Pard.

But Pard took their sudden hounding in stride. "I just realized it myself. Basically..." Her eyes flicked over to the only person who hadn't cried out—Aqua Current.

Handed the baton, Akira simply circulated her flowing water armor for a while, but finally, she murmured, "I don't really want to say it."

"What? You knew as well, Curren? ...Mm...Oh...I see. So is that it...?" As she spoke, Kuroyukihime apparently came to understand something, crossed her arms, and abruptly fell silent.

This was followed by Fuko, Utai, and Niko all murmuring "Oh..."

And then, for some reason, even Takumu and Chiyuri were muttering, "No way..." and "Perhaps..." until finally, it was only Haruyuki left in the not-understanding zone. Trying to escape from this too-sad situation, he frantically set his mind to work.

A method of reselecting level-up bonuses. Aqua Current had known about it for a long time. Blood Leopard realized it recently. The common point between the two with regard to leveling up was...

"Oh! R-right!" When he finally reached this place, a simple answer flashed in the back of his mind, and Haruyuki cried out. The commonality was not leveling up, but leveling *down*: the God Seiryu's unique attack, Level Drain.

While everyone there hesitated to say it out loud, Akira nodded, arcs of flowing water shimmering. "Yes. When you drop levels in Seiryu's attack, the bonuses you got with the relevant levels also disappear. Put another way, when you reach that level again, you can reselect your bonus."

"B-but, Curren." Haruyuki took a step forward and gave voice to one of the many questions that popped up into his mind. "When you were at level one, you still had lots of abilities, right?"

In addition to the Hydro Auditory she revealed in the Territories the previous day, which turned all of a stage's water into her own personal sound system, Aqua Current had a group of abilities such as being able to slide down water surfaces and envelop companions in her water armor, an impossible diversity for a level one.

"I didn't get those abilities through level-up bonuses," Akira replied smoothly. "Just like your Aviation and Optical Conduction, they came to me suddenly in the middle of battle. So they didn't go away even after I leveled down."

"Ohhh..." Haruyuki let out a large sigh of admiration.

Aqua Current had long worked as the bouncer to protect newbie Linkers on the verge of total point loss and had also been given the nickname The One, with the idea that she was the most powerful level one in the Accelerated World. Haruyuki himself had once been saved by her in a pinch. This strength of hers had been refined precisely because she had endured the terrifying adversity of the level drop.

Entire body dyed the color of the evening sun, the flowing water avatar looked around at the others. "The reason I didn't explain the secondary effects of Level Drain before," she said in a tone slightly more clipped than usual, "is because I didn't want you to decide to fight Seiryu in order to reselect level-up bonuses. I think you all noticed this in the mission there, but unless a fixed period of time passes in the battle—or more likely, it gets angry for real—my impression is that Seiryu doesn't use Level Drain. If you go for an easy fight, there's a fairly strong possibility you'll die before you get to that stage. It's totally impossible to just set foot on the bridge, get your level lowered, and then make a quick getaway."

"Mm, that's exactly right," Kuroyukihime said. "But it's all right, Curren. Not a soul here regrets their own choices. And Leopard, you can't be saying that you'd really and deliberately go for level down."

Pard nodded, almost as if to say "of course." "Y. I mentioned the possibility of bonus reselection because I wanted Current to tell us this. My short temper's one thing, but, Curren, you need to fix this habit of holding everything in."

"..."

Her child held nothing back in letting her know what was what, and Akira let a hint of a wry laugh bleed across the water covering her face mask. "I'll try. I'm still holding onto all kinds of things, but I'll tell you bit by bit."

"K." Pard took a step back from the tower wall and tossed Niko from the crook of her arm high up into the air directly above her.

"Whaaaaa?!" The Red King, likely the lightest avatar there, flew up into space, screaming.

"Shape Change." Once she had transformed from human to leopard, she caught Niko on her back.

"Uh, so, Pard, you just said you were going to work on your impatience!" her Legion Master shrieked.

"Work target," Pard replied, setting her right now-front paw, after the Change, to tap on the tower wall. After pressing the pads of that paw against it a few times, she nodded as if satisfied and then smoothly climbed the vertical surface about three meters up. Panicking, Niko, on her back, grabbed at her neck.

"K. I can prob'ly make it to the top."

"P-prob'ly?!"

"…Most likely."

"M-most likely?!"

The two members of the Red Legion went back and forth, a perfectly timed comedic duo.

"Roger." Fuko waved and smiled. "Then we'll see you at the top."

"K." Pard began to run up the slick marble wall. Running up a wall didn't look all that extravagant, but it was a relatively rare and powerful ability. And combined with Blood Leopard's inherent agility, it was basically the same as there being no obstacles in a stage.

Eeeaaaah! Niko's voice—maybe a scream, maybe a cheer—receded, and once they could no longer hear it, Fuko smiled happily.

"…Prominence's increased their power quite a bit with this, hmm? I'm really looking forward to the day when our Legions fight."

"Mm-hmm. We also must get stronger for that," Kuroyuki-hime responded, bringing her gaze back to earth. "Now then, we should go, too. Who will you carry, Raker?"

"Goodness! You have to ask?" Fuko spread her hands out slightly as if to indicate that it went without saying, and then suddenly vanished from the wheelchair. With a speed on par with teleportation, she had moved directly behind Utai. The small shrine maiden's face stiffened and she tried to leap away, but two hands yanked her off the ground.

"Auunh, I—I was careless." Utai's arms and legs hung limply, as though she had resigned herself to her fate of being a tightly held sack of potatoes.

"It's all right, Maiden," Fuko declared lovingly. "I won't drop you or anything today."

"O-of course you will not!"

Kuroyukihime shook her head in exasperation at the seasoned duo of ICBM and Testarossa—and their act so reminiscent of the two members of the Red Legion—and then turned back to Haru-yuki. "Which means, Crow, that you end up carrying Pile, Bell, Curren, and me. So? Can you do it in one go?"

"Yes, that's okay!" Haruyuki bobbed his head up and down, while Chiyuri looked on slightly skeptical. But this time, his promise was not baseless and ill-conceived. During the mission to subjugate the fifth Chrome Disaster six months earlier, Haru-yuki had flown nonstop the five kilometers from Suginami to Ikebukuro with Black Lotus under his right arm, Scarlet Rain in his left, and Cyan Pile hanging from his legs.

This time, there was the addition of Aqua Current, and Lime Bell was a bit heavier than Rain, but as long as he didn't go too fast, he should have been able to lift four people at once over a distance of three hundred meters.

"Okay then, Lotus, we'll go on ahead." Holding Utai in front of her, Fuko stored her wheelchair and summoned Gale Thruster, waved her right hand in the air, and then looked up at the sky. She bent her knees and jumped lightly while at the same time igniting the boosters. Glittering with a blue light, the flames of propulsion immediately receded into the twilight.

"Now, shall we go as well?" As she spoke, Kuroyukihime brought her body close to Haruyuki's right arm.

This was, of course, not their first tandem flight, but when he touched his beloved swordmaster, even though they were both avatars, his heart pounded as usual. Still, he managed to smoothly lift her by her narrow waist, and breathing a sigh of relief to himself, he stretched out his left hand to Chiyuri. "C'mon, Chiyu. Hurry up."

"You are weirdly used to this."

"I—I am not! I—I—I don't care if you hang from my legs instead!"

"Yeah, yeah. Fine. Please and thank you." Chiyuri leaned— almost slammed—into him.

Once he had his left arm around her, this time without any excessive heart pounding, Haruyuki had a sudden thought: *If Takumu grabbed onto his legs like last time, how would he hang onto Aqua Current?*

"It's fine," Akira said, as if reading his thoughts. She approached from the front to wrap both her arms around his neck. Before he had a chance to panic and freak out, the water film covering Current's entire body was adhered to Crow's silver armor; it was probably an application of her ability to slide down walls. In which case, even if Haruyuki didn't support her, she likely wouldn't fall.

After securing the three on his upper body, Haruyuki spread his wings and vibrated them carefully. He slowly left the ground and went into a hover about a meter and a half in the air. "You're good, Taku. Sorry for putting you on the bottom all the time."

Cyan Pile grabbed on tightly right away from behind—or he should have, but there was no response, so Haruyuki called to him once more. "Taku?"

"Oh. Right, sorry, Haru. Thanks." This time, there was a response, and the sturdy arms wrapped tightly around both of Silver Crow's legs.

Haruyuki gradually increased his thrust until Cyan Pile's legs were off the ground and then turned his eyes upward.

Fuko and Utai had morphed into a missile and shot upward so quickly that they were already out of sight, but he still could spot a small shadow moving along the wall high up in the distance. It looked like Pard was also going to make it to the top without her ability's effect running out midway.

"Okay, here we go!" Haruyuki called, increasing the frequency of his silver wings' vibration.

Vwwm! A sense of gravity akin to the departure of an elevator came over him and then quickly changed into a floating sensation. Maintaining a distance of five meters or so from the tower wall, he ascended at a fixed speed. His special-attack gauge started to drop in the upper left of his field of view, but as long as he stuck to eco-flying mode, it looked like it would last long enough.

"Wow!" Chiyuri let out a cry of delight. "There's, like, all these temples over there! Haru, move a little to the left!"

"Uh, um, so…if my gauge runs out, use Citron Call." Grumbling, Haruyuki moved horizontally from the south side to the west. While he was at it, he turned his body to the left, and the center of Twilight-stage Tokyo spread out before him.

To his right, he could see a vast space encircled by a bottomless pit—the Castle where the fierce battle with Seiryu had only just played out. But Chiyuri was likely talking about the group of high-rise temples standing in a row in front of that. The floors supported by (probably) Corinthian columns were stacked in several layers, so that the whole thing looked like a future city in the style of ancient Greece.

In the face of the magnificent panorama, Haruyuki forgot to even complain, and as he gazed at the view, Kuroyukihime stretched out the sword of her right arm.

"That area is Kasumigaseki and Nagatacho. From the right, it's the Ministry of Finance; the Ministry of Agriculture; Forestry and Fisheries; and the Cabinet Office. The short, large one beyond that is the National Diet Building. Didn't you go there on a social studies field trip in elementary?"

"Oh! We did!" Chiyuri beat him to the punch. "We did go! Haru got lost inside, and it turned into this whole thing!"

This was confidential information his childhood friend was spilling, so Haruyuki hurriedly tried to fix it. "I—I wasn't lost! I was exploring! There's a secret room in the Capitol Building in the US, so I just figured maybe there was one in the Diet Building in Japan…"

"That's from a movie we watched way back when! There aren't any secret rooms in the US or in Japan!"

"How can you be so sure?! It's a secret! They keep it hidden from the people!"

"No way. You believe that?! Even now, in eighth grade?!"

"Wh-whatever! It's fine! There's no age limit on imagination!"

Haruyuki and Chiyuri continued to bicker and ruin the hard-won view, when abruptly, a giggle slipped out of Current, pressed up against his chest.

"Truly, a very Crow episode. I apologize for destroying the mood, but I think there is perhaps a way to check if there actually is or isn't a secret room."

"What?! D-do you mean sneak in?"

Now it was Kuroyukihime's turn to laugh at the dumbfounded Haruyuki. "Is that it? I see. Check in the Accelerated World rather than the real? If there are social cameras in this secret room or what have you, then it would be generated on this side as well. The building structural changes in the Twilight stage are extreme, but, right…if it were a Factory stage or a Steel stage…"

"Oh, I get it! Okay, so let's go check it out on our next day off!"

"What?! You just denied the whole idea a minute ago!"

And so they went on. Haruyuki continued to gain altitude at a fixed pace, and finally, the Castle and the National Diet Building were hidden beneath thin clouds. Turning his gaze skyward once again, he saw the edge of the tower now cut a clean curve into the twilight sky. The four who had gone ahead had presumably already landed; he could see no sign of them.

As expected, it looked like he'd have a little extra in his special-attack gauge, so he sped up for the last thirty meters and flew over the old Tokyo Tower. Just as he remembered, the top was covered by a lush, grassy garden, and he saw Fuko and the others in one corner.

"Sorry to keep you waiting!" Haruyuki called out to the four who had arrived ahead of them as he halted his ascent and shifted to gliding. First, Takumu, dangling below, let go and landed with a thump on the lawn. Then, when Haruyuki just barely stuck his landing, Kuroyukihime and the others jumped down from his arms and chest, and offered their own words of thanks.

His role as transport carrier completed without incident, Haruyuki let out a long breath and then abruptly realized Takumu had been excessively quiet during the flight. *Maybe he's no good with heights*, he thought as he moved to look at his friend behind him, but Fuko's voice interrupted him.

"Everyone, welcome to my garden. This is the first time I've had so many guests. I hope we all fit inside the house."

Now that she mentioned it, Fuko's house, where Haruyuki himself had once stayed—which had apparently been given the elegant name Fufuan—was not as big a structure as all that. Would nine people actually fit in there? Haruyuki had his gaze turned to the circular space of the garden, and then suddenly opened his eyes wide.

In the center of the garden was a small pond. And in the center of the water, an elliptical shape shimmering blue on the water surface, shining orange as it reflected the evening sun—a portal. So far, this was all as he remembered. But the neat cottage with the green roof and white walls that should have been on the other side of the pond was not there, no matter how he strained his eyes.

Haruyuki forgot Takumu's strange silence and pointed to the

east side of the garden. "Uh! Um! Master! Y-your house is— The house isn't there!"

"Hee-hee-hee." Fuko, who had already taken off Gale Thruster and returned to her usual white dress form, laughed, the broad brim of her hat shaking. "It's not as though it was blown away by a tornado or destroyed by a wolf. A locked player home doesn't materialize unless the owner approaches it."

Deftly flicking through her Instruct menu, she turned a small item into an object. In her hand, shining with a silver light, was an old-fashioned key.

Now that he thought about it, Haruyuki himself had feverishly searched for a key that had long been sleeping in a corner of the Unlimited Neutral Field a mere nine days ago in order to access a player home somewhere else. He had left it inside the main room, together with two high-level Enhanced Armaments, so no one would ever be able to find the house again.

With a key of a different shape than the one Haruyuki had found, Fuko took a few steps toward the pond. When she did, the familiar white cottage appeared, wrapped in a hazy light.

"Ooh!" Chiyuri and Niko cooed in awe.

"Now please come this way." Fuko turned around and beckoned them with a wave. "I'm sure I have some food left. Although, they might be a thousand years or so past their expiration dates."

4

Suddenly, Haruyuki felt like he'd heard a faint sound. He opened his eyes a crack and saw the lone door being closed. Someone had left the room.

Lifting his head slightly, he looked around. His comrades were scattered around on the floor of Fufuan, which was larger than he had remembered, all asleep for the time being. And naturally, all still duel avatars.

Niko was using Pard, who was curled up like a cat, as a pillow. Lying on her side, Fuko was holding Utai tightly in her arms. Shuddering and flickering beside them was Akira, her flowing water armor rolled up in a ball. Takumu was asleep with his back against the wall, and Chiyuri had her arms and legs splayed out next to Haruyuki.

But there was no one in the room's only bed.

The right to use the bed had been unanimously presented to the Black King, who looked like she would have trouble sleeping on the floor, given her variously tapered form. Which meant it had been Kuroyukihime who had left the house seconds earlier. If they had been in the real world, he could have brushed this off with the question "Bathroom, maybe?" but in the Accelerated World, no matter how much you ate or drank, no such physical needs were generated.

"…"

After wrestling with his sleepiness for a few more seconds, Haruyuki slowly sat up. He stood, being careful not to make a sound, and then stealthily tiptoed across the wooden floor. When he touched the doorknob, the door opened outward, and he slipped through and closed it carefully. Perhaps the sound he'd heard before was the whisper of wind sneaking in during the door's opening and closing.

Outside the house, the world was still wrapped in the same vivid dusky light as when they'd arrived. When he checked the continuous dive time in his Instruct menu, it seemed that he'd been asleep for about five hours, but apparently, the Change had not come during that time.

He made the menu disappear and looked around to find a silhouette sitting on the bench at the western edge of the tower's outer circumference. From where Haruyuki was standing, it overlapped perfectly with the red evening sun floating on the horizon. The sharp form of the black silhouette was nothing less than heroic on the battlefield, but it now felt ephemeral for some reason, like art made of glass, and Haruyuki stared soundlessly in that direction for a while. The wind blew up again, causing faint ripples on the surface of the pond, and this spurred him to start walking.

Perhaps she had already noticed that Haruyuki had been the one to come out of the house. "Sorry. Did I wake you?" Kuroyuki-hime asked quietly, once he'd gotten about two meters away from the bench.

"…No, I slept plenty already."

Without a word, the young woman slid over to the right. Haruyuki took another five steps to come around to the front of the bench from the left, and then set himself down in the empty space. The garden in the sky dropped off close ahead, and there were no handrails or anything at the edge, so when he lifted his face, a spectacular view of the Accelerated World spread out before him. Not only could he see the central areas from Roppongi to Shibuya, but he could see the city beyond that, continuing out to Setagaya, Chofu, and Hachioji, and even farther out, where the mountains of Okutama were illuminated by the eternal twilight sun, burning red. He felt like his heart almost pulled into the scene.

"It would feel so good if I could just fly and fly and fly toward that sun with you," Kuroyukihime murmured.

"I...guess so. I feel like right now, we could make it to the end of the Accelerated World," he responded half-consciously, before suddenly coming back to himself and adding, "although my gauge would actually run out somewhere around Shibuya."

"What if you used the Incarnate System, I wonder," Kuroyukihime added after a brief silence.

"What...?" Haruyuki glanced over, but just like Crow's, the Black King's face was hidden by full-cover goggles, and he couldn't discern her expression. He returned his gaze to the setting sun in the distance and thought a little before replying. "Um. If I kept climbing as high as I could with Light Speed and then gliding, I think we could go pretty far. But that's the least stable of my Incarnate techniques. I practice sometimes, but there are plenty of times when my imagination's lacking and I can't activate it."

"I see...No, it was just a random thought. I'm sorry for suggesting something so suspect. The activation of Incarnate techniques is largely connected with your mental state. So it's not always going to go the way you want in regular training. No need to rush it."

"R-right." Haruyuki nodded, but something still wasn't quite clicking for him, and he snuck a peek at her face in profile once more. The Incarnate System had a dual nature, light and dark. For instance, even if it was a positive Incarnate technique, taking hope as its energy source, if you misused it, you would be pulled toward the hole in your heart and eventually swallowed up by a bottomless darkness. It was Kuroyukihime herself who had taught him this, and she had barely ever said the word *Incarnate* without referencing its drawbacks.

Unable to get the question "What's wrong?" out of his mouth, Haruyuki sat in silence.

Abruptly, Kuroyukihime moved her left hand and opened the Instruct menu. She deftly selected commands and categories on a screen that looked invisible to Haruyuki and apparently pulled something out of her storage. White particles of light collected in her hand and came together in the shape of a small rectangle.

It was a familiar object in the Accelerated World—an item card. They held sealed within them all kinds of consumables, Armaments, burst points, and more, while others still had their own special functions like replay cards or sudden-death duel cards.

Straining his eyes to see exactly what this particular card was, Haruyuki immediately inhaled sharply beneath his goggles. This thing sitting at the tip of Kuroyukihime's sword had a string of vivid-red characters on an inky matte-black backdrop. Even from where he was sitting, he could read the English text inscribed there. INCARNATE SYSTEM STUDY KIT. It was the sealed ISS kit card he'd obtained four days earlier in the Setagaya area.

An F-type Burst Linker by the name of Magenta Scissor had given it to him. She was planning to homogenize the Accelerated World with the ISS kits, and she had tried to get the small, three-member Legion Petit Paquet under her control. But she had given up when Silver Crow and Lime Bell had intervened, and then handed the two now-unnecessary sealed cards to Haruyuki before she'd left.

It wasn't that Magenta had abandoned her plan to disseminate the kits. That was clear from the fact that a mere three days later, she had attacked Ash Roller in Setagaya Area No. 1 and forcibly infected him with a kit. But then why had she given the two sealed cards to Haruyuki? She herself said they were tainted with positive Incarnate, so she could no longer use them, but in that case, she could have just destroyed them herself or left them to lie around in storage.

Of course, there was also the possibility that it was some kind of trap, but Haruyuki just couldn't believe that. He'd sensed a kind of pride in Magenta Scissor's back as she left the cards and departed after losing a fierce battle. A strong will that said she definitely wasn't just being manipulated by the ISS kit—or by its makers, the Acceleration Research Society.

Thus, Haruyuki had taken the two cards home, and at the meeting the next day, he showed them to Kuroyukihime and Fuko. Naturally, they were both surprised, but the reason for that went beyond anything Haruyuki could have imagined. A single crest was hidden on the jet-black background of the ISS kit card. The crest of the first Red King, the Master Gunsmith, Red Rider.

Having materialized the sealed card, Kuroyukihime held it above her head as she had three days earlier, up to the setting sun of the Twilight stage. Behind the item name, the crossed-guns crest rose up. The sword tip the card was adhered to shook for an instant. The air grew tense, telling the story of Kuroyukihime's deep pain.

Thinking that this time, for sure, he had to say something, Haruyuki opened his mouth in a trance and called to her. "Kuroyukihime..."

She glanced over at him. But the words that should have followed did not come.

"Um...Uh..." Panicking slightly, Haruyuki blurted out a question that was definitely inappropriate for the moment, despite the dozens of things he could have said. "H-how do you get items to stick to your sword? Is it like a magnet or something?"

"Mm...?" This was no doubt outside her expectations, and she blinked her eye lenses a few times before she replied with a wry smile. "No, there aren't magnets in there or anything. In my perception, I'm definitely holding it with my fingertips, but you just can't see those fingers...Something like that, I guess..."

"H-huh...So then, like, typing on a keyboard..."

"Mm, it's not impossible. Although it *is* a trial since I can't see my fingers. In the Incarnate technique I showed you before, where I turn my sword into a hand, I am the source imagining my fingers becoming one with the sword. Like your Light Speed, though, it won't really stabilize..."

She stopped there for a moment, and then continued, sounding as though she were peering into the distant past on the other side of the card.

"...A long, long time ago, Rider said...'You couldn't shoot me even if I did give you one of my guns, Lotus.' I was a child, I thought he was teasing me, so I took offense...But maybe he was already planning it at that time. The Seven Roads, guns that absolutely could not be fired on the Seven Kings. Giving us those symbols of eternal friendship and peace. And in the end, right up to the last, he never knew this hand actually *could* shoot a gun..."

"...Kuroyukihime..." Once again, all Haruyuki could do was call her name.

But she nodded deeply at him and lowered the card. "...You went to the trouble of bringing this sealed card back for us, but I haven't been able to uncover the reason why Rider's crest is inscribed on it. And it goes without saying that I can't try opening the seal."

"O-of course not! Please don't say something like that, even as a joke."

"Yes, right. Nonetheless, we still know nothing about the card itself. But I feel like I can more or less imagine Magenta Scissor's intention in giving it to you."

"Huh? Wh-what do you mean...?"

"She knows that the crest hidden on the card is Red Rider's and that I was the one who pushed Rider to total point loss. And she also assumed you would show me the card once you had it. In other words, this is a challenge to me. Magenta is asking me if I'm prepared to face head-on the ISS kit main body and whatever relationship it has with Rider."

"...!!" At these utterly unexpected words, Haruyuki's entire

body stiffened again. "Th-that's— So then I did exactly what Magenta..."

"No, I'm not reproaching you. It was the right decision to give me the card. Thanks to that, I was able to tell you about the White King, something I haven't been able to speak about all this time...And I was able to gain some time to ready myself before the attack on Midtown Tower. In that sense, I almost have to thank Magenta."

"......"

Although Kuroyukihime was kind enough to reassure him like this, he couldn't actually hold his head up high for a while. Whatever Magenta Scissor's true intent, it was a fact that Haruyuki had given Kuroyukihime an enormous mental shock. Head hanging deeply, he murmured, *I'm sorry, Kuroyukihime* in his heart, and then took a deep breath and switched gears. If she was trying to ready herself, then he couldn't shake her up now.

"...Kuroyukihime?" Yanking himself up straight, Haruyuki voiced the biggest question that had popped up during their conversation so far. "What do you think the 'whatever relationship' you mentioned between Red Rider and the ISS kit main body *is*? The first Red King left the Accelerated World a long time ago, more than two and a half years ago. I don't think it's possible for him to be directly involved..."

"Mm...I think you're quite right. If any relationship is possible, then the only thing I can imagine is that some kind of Enhanced Armament generated with Rider's unique ability—with Arms Creation—is still somewhere in the Accelerated World, and that it's playing a role in the production of the ISS kits."

"Arms...Creation..." As he hoarsely parroted the words, Haruyuki was once again struck by how incredible an ability this power of the first Red King's actually was.

Normally, Enhanced Armament could only be obtained through level-up bonuses or purchases at the shop, but Red Rider had been able to *make* them. The true wonder of this power was in the way it grew in influence the more time passed. Even assuming he could only make one every three days, that was ten weap-ons in a month. Which worked out to a pile of a hundred twenty guns in a year. He didn't have to think too hard to see how much these arms would strengthen the Legion.

So then, rather than stopping at mere guns, did Red Rider go even further and produce some *thing* that could make new Enhanced Armaments? And then, through whatever set of cir-cumstances, did that *thing* fall into the hands of the Acceleration Research Society, and was it now being used to manufacture ISS kits?

"An Enhanced Armament that can generate Enhanced Arma-ments..." Kuroyukihime nodded slightly, as if Haruyuki had spoken these thoughts out loud. "If you'd asked me four days ago whether something like that could exist, I would have laughed it off. But now that I've seen Rider's crest inscribed on the sealed ISS kit card...I can't think of any other explanation. And..."

Kuroyukihime cut herself off there and turned her face mask to the right of the evening sun. Ahead, skyscrapers soared upward, a little shorter than the old Tokyo Tower but several times wider. Two buildings, with the wide main road between them. The curvy building on the left was Roppongi Hills Tower, where Haruyuki had once fought the Green King, Green Grandé. And the perfectly square building to the right was Tokyo Midtown Tower, the ultimate target of their current mission. Kuroyuki-hime's eye lenses were naturally turned to the tower on the right. Like the other buildings in the stage, it had been transformed to resemble a chalky temple, but even from twelve hundred meters away, Haruyuki felt a kind of unearthliness shrouding it.

Encamped at the summit of Midtown Tower was the Legend-class Enemy Archangel Metatron, invisible and impenetrable to all attacks, and its eyes shone with a light that would generally evaporate anyone who came within two hundred meters of the building. And on one of the higher floors hid the ISS kit main body, the core of the Acceleration Research Society's plans. Unless they succeeded in their task to slip past Metatron's ferocious attack, charge into the tower, and destroy the kit main body, the Accelerated World would be blanketed in darkness—and Haruyuki would lose his bond with Rin Kusakabe and Ash Roller forever.

He unconsciously curled his hands into tight fists, and Kuroyukihime began to speak once more as she stared at Midtown Tower. "And I feel it. Like, I'm going to end up facing my past in that place...Although I don't know yet what form it will take."

"Your...past?"

"Yes. Since becoming a Burst Linker seven years ago, I've made a great many mistakes. Driven forward by my endless ambition, I have brandished my swords and spilled much blood. This card is wet with that blood. If I can reach that puddle of it...At the source, my past is most certainly waiting for me."

Uttering these bleak words, Kuroyukihime sat up straighter, her eyes still on the massive tower in the distance. "But I won't forget anymore. I'm not going to try to run from the past. I have Fuko, Utai, Akira, Takumu, Chiyuri, Niko, Leopard...and you. No matter what is waiting there in the tower, I will not take even a single step back. That alone I promise you now."

Even after she stopped speaking, Haruyuki couldn't respond right away. In fact, he couldn't even turn his head. Because the tears that had built up beneath his silver mask threatened to spill out if he moved even a little.

Staring hard at the evening sun, blurred into a rainbow, Haruyuki took a deep breath and somehow managed to reply. "I... promise, too. No matter how hard the fight is, I won't break. I won't give up. I will fight with you, by your side right up until the last."

"Mm." Kuroyukihime nodded and then, after a second, added, "But if I tell you to run—"

"I'm not leaving you and everyone and running. Never," Haruyuki declared resolutely before she could finish.

*　　*　　*

In the end, Haruyuki and Kuroyukihime didn't go back to Fufuan, but rather stayed there, talking on the bench. Ninety percent of their conversation was meaningless chatter, but recently, Kuroyukihime had been busy preparing for the school festival, and they hadn't really had time to talk, just the two of them, so for Haruyuki, it was a span of time like a dream.

Eventually, he heard the door opening behind them and looked back to see Niko stepping out on the grass, stretching hard. She froze when she noticed him sitting alongside Kuroyukihime, and her two antennas twitched and shivered before she came over to them at a trot.

"Morning, Big Brother! ♪"

Why angel mode all of a sudden? His guard up, Haruyuki returned the greeting. "M-morning, Niko. You sleep okay?"

"Yup! But my big brother was supposed to be snuggling me, and when I woke up, he was gone, so I was saaaad."

"...Oh?"

He heard a fairly severe voice beside him, and Haruyuki waved both hands and shook his head frantically from side to side as he leapt off the bench.

"N-no, no, no, no!" Yelping, he turned back to Niko and hastily retreated several steps—until one of his feet missed the edge of the tower, and he lurched backward.

"Wh-whoa, whoa, whoa!" He flung out his arms, flailing, before he finally remembered the wings on his back and fluttered them slightly to return to solid ground. He panted heavily before insisting, "I—I wasn't hugging you! You were using Pard as a pillow the whole time!"

"Oh my? Waaaas I? Oh, I know! ♪ I was getting my memory of last night mixed up with—"

"Aaaaah!" Haruyuki made an enormous *X* with his arms to shut Niko up, and then cleared his throat several times, straightened again, and deliberately changed the topic. "A-anyway, is everyone else still asleep, then? Given that we still need time for the strategy meeting, maybe it's about time we woke them!"

"Oh, Raker was awake, so she probably woke everyone else up by now. But, like, did you guys actually get any sleep?"

At this question from Niko—angel mode ended—Kuroyukihime nodded, some suspicion still hanging in the air around her. "Yes, no problems. We woke up a little early, so we were merely examining attack strategies."

"Ohhh, *attack* strategies, hmm?"

"...What are you trying to say?"

"Noooothing."

Sparks crackled in the air between the two kings—or they did in Haruyuki's mind anyway. He started to retreat again, but only a fool would step off the edge a second time.

"Uh, um." He managed to still his feet and speak. "S-so then, I'll go call everyone else. I figure it's probably better to have the meeting looking at Midtown Tower."

Taking care to move with the utmost naturalness, he had taken a few steps when he heard Kuroyukihime's voice behind him.

"Haruyuki. Once the mission is complete and we return to the other side, I would like to ask you about *last night*, so stay in the student council office."

".....H-hokay," he replied nervously, then headed for the house at a quick pace somewhere between a fast walk and a trot.

On the other side of the still-open door, everyone was awake and up just as Niko had guessed. Only Pard and Akira, who were apparently not morning people, were a bit unsteady on their feet, but they came out with Fuko prodding them forward.

Utai, Chiyuri, and Takumu followed shortly after, and no sooner was the house empty than Fuko was immediately closing the door and locking it.

She's really on top of it, Haruyuki thought.

She looked back, key dangling in her right hand. "We don't even use this kind of key in the real world, what with long-distance locks for houses and cars. So if I don't lock it right after I come outside, I forget."

"Oh, makes sense. Have you ever actually forgotten?"

"I have, of course. I went without realizing I'd forgotten to lock it for five days in real time. I left the door wide open for nearly fourteen years on this side."

"F-fourteen…Did any robbers or anyone come inside?"

"It really was quite strange. Although the items I'd put into the storage attached to the house were all fine, the food alone was completely gone. I think it was Ash's work, but he wouldn't confess even when I questioned him."

Haruyuki started to imagine exactly what form the questioning took before he had an abrupt realization and shook his head violently. "Oh! N-no, it wasn't me either!"

"Goodness, you weren't even asked the question yet. That's quite the quick reaction, hmm?"

"I—I—I—I—I—I really didn't!"

Ahead of them, Akira and Pard were apparently back to normal blood pressure, awake enough now to both turn at the same time.

"Def a ghost."

"You should have it exorcised right away."

"Ha-ha! There aren't any ghosts in the Accelerated World," Haruyuki said, laughing.

Fuko exchanged looks with Pard and Akira, and then smiled in a profoundly meaningful way.

"Huh? Th-there are…?"

Instead of answering, the three older girls stepped briskly toward the other side of the pond.

"Uh! Um! Hey! Please tell me!" Even as he chased after them in a panic, Haruyuki was whirling his head around, looking at his surroundings.

Once all nine were together by the side of the pond, Kuroyuki-hime opened her Instruct menu once more and checked the cumulative dive time.

"As of this moment, ten hours have passed. Unfortunately, I suppose, there has been no Change. The Twilight stage will continue for the time being. These are slightly, but only slightly, disadvantageous conditions for fighting Metatron. But as we also discussed at school, right from the start, it is an impossibility to defeat that Legend-class Enemy in anything other than a Hell stage. We have one objective: break into Midtown Tower and destroy the ISS kit main body. Ultimately, we would ignore Metatron, were it possible. Is there anything else to note so far?"

"Yes." Takumu raised his right hand—well, his pile driver. "Master, this is just in case, but...Will Metatron stop attacking once we enter the tower?"

"Mm...That is a point of concern, it's true." Kuroyukihime turned and looked out at the building in question, rising twelve hundred meters to the northwest. "We can't see it right now, but Metatron is camped out on the top of that building. And it uses its insta-death laser attack on anyone who comes within two hundred meters. Correct so far, yes, Crow?"

She looked to Haruyuki for confirmation, and he nodded deeply.

"Yes. I saw Metatron on the roof with my own eyes, although just its silhouette. And also how it evaporated anything that came into its territory with this immensely powerful laser. Two hundred meters was what GW's Iron Pound told me. Pound said Midtown Tower was a 'tiny Castle.'"

"Hmm, that is well said, hmm?" Chuckling, Fuko shifted her gaze from the enormous tower in the distance to Haruyuki and cocked her head slightly to one side. "Corvus, you said 'anything that came into its territory' just now. Does that perhaps mean it's not just Burst Linkers but any object that will get shot down with the laser?"

"Uh...Um..." Haruyuki sank into thought.

"Oh, I got it!" Chiyuri cried out. "If Metatron will shoot anything, then we can throw rocks and stuff from outside its range and make it shoot its laser for no reason and use up all its energy, right, Sis?"

"Yes. It might be a Legend-class Enemy, but it's not as though it has an infinite energy source. If we can make it fire persistently, that source should be exhausted at some point. Well then, Corvus?"

The center of everyone's attention, Haruyuki lifted his face and slowly shook his head. "No...It's too bad, but I don't think we can do that. When I was shown Metatron's laser, Pound deliberately used his own arm as bait. And that rocket punch, once it's broken, he's like that until he leaves the stage, right?" He saw Fuko nod and continued, "So then if rocks or something would have done the trick, he would have used his arm. Which means, at the very least, Metatron won't fire its laser unless part of a duel avatar comes within the two-hundred-meter range..."

"Mm, I see...What was the time delay like, from the moment it reacted to the intruder until it actually fired the laser?" Kuroyukihime asked.

"Um." Haruyuki again replayed the movie from ten days earlier in the back of his mind. "The rocket punch crossed the expressway and then got closer to Midtown Tower...And then a transparent *something* moved on the top of the tower. It spread these incredibly huge wings, and the wings kind of lit up. And by the time I noticed that, the laser was firing. So from reaction to firing...Right, at most it would have been about two seconds."

"Two seconds...It would indeed be difficult to make it across two hundred meters before being fired upon."

Everyone nodded at Kuroyukihime's words.

Haruyuki felt like it maybe wasn't impossible for Fuko alone to use her booster one way and fly at top speed to reach the building. But they didn't know what was waiting inside Midtown Tower. It was hard to believe that the thoroughly prepared Acceleration Research Society would have left guarding the ISS kit main body to Metatron alone. So even if she did succeed in reaching the tower, they could expect more fighting inside, making a lone charge far more dangerous.

If it had been the Haruyuki from a little while ago, he would have said something reckless and foolish now, like, "It's all right...I'll go alone." But having come through a tumultuous month, Haruyuki had learned that if there were times when you had to fight alone, there were also times when you needed to lean on your friends.

Thus, as he stepped into the center of the circle they made, Haruyuki said calmly, "It's all right. I'll make sure to defend against Metatron's laser until you all reach the tower."

For a moment, none of the others reacted to this, but rather simply stared at him. He started to worry he'd said something stupid yet again.

"We do appreciate your effort, C," Utai declared, and then everyone else was talking all in a jumble.

"Thanks, Haru!"

"We're counting on you, 'kay!"

"I know you will."

"I'm trusting you here!"

"Please do."

"We'll leave it to you, Corvus."

And then finally, Kuroyukihime nodded heavily. "Now again, after the Seiryu fight, we are placing a heavy burden on your shoulders. But, Crow, I believe your wings are exactly the thing that is going to break through to the future of Nega Nebulus and the Accelerated World. To destroy the ISS kit main body and clear away the darkness that is trying to fall over the world...and to save our dear friend, lend me your strength."

"My strength has always belonged to you, Black King. Just give the order, and I will fly to any height."

"I see. Well, then..." Turning toward Haruyuki and advancing, Kuroyukihime stretched the sword of her right hand out. The sharp tip was lit with a soft overlay, and in the next instant, the blade split without a sound to create five fingers. Everyone except

Haruyuki gasped, while Kuroyukihime, rather than giving an order, said softly, "Let's fight. Together."

"...Okay!" Haruyuki gently gripped the slender "hand" proffered.

Previously, Kuroyukihime had only been able to maintain the adapted Incarnate technique, with no attack power whatsoever, for a maximum of about twenty seconds. But once she released Haruyuki's hand, she shook the hands of the other seven in order. Immediately after she had released Fuko's, the last, there was a sharp *ting!* and the five fingers turned back into a sword. The hand had shattered before instead of turning back, so it wasn't just the time she had made progress with.

Akira, Utai, and Fuko, who had known Kuroyukihime the longest, must have been impressed. And even after Kuroyukihime returned to her original position, she continued to stare down at her own hand for a while.

"If Lotus is gonna go that far on us, we gotta throw ourselves into it, too!" Niko cried quite forcefully on behalf of the speechless members of Nega Nebulus. "Up against an Enemy, no need to hold back. We'll send it flying, Incarnate guns blazing right from the start!"

Yeah! The cheering voices sent gentle ripples across the pond beside them.

They took an hour or so for a briefing and nailed down the details of their charge on Midtown Tower. When it was finally five minutes before their scheduled departure, Haruyuki had a sudden thought and moved over to the western edge of the garden once more. He stared intently at the view of Minato Ward spreading out below him. He had only looked at the area around Midtown Tower when he was sitting on the bench with Kuroyukihime, but he remembered now that there was also another place he ought to be burning into his brain.

Minato was somewhere he normally never went, so he had even less of a sense of the place than he did of Shibuya. But he sort of spread out a map of Tokyo in the back of his mind and overlaid it on the terrain of the Twilight stage. The wide road cutting across the southern side of the old Tokyo Tower was Ring Road No. 3. On the other side of this was Azabu, with its many embassies from all kinds of countries. Even farther to the south was Minato Ward's Shirokane, which Haruyuki basically knew only as the name of a ritzy residential area.

He peered at the Shirokane area where small temple ruins were clustered—although in the real world, they were likely palatial mansions—and saw a fairly large open space in the center. In terms of area, it was closing in on the size of Shiba Park, which sat at the base of old Tokyo Tower's east side. Still, within the site stood a group of large temples with room to spare between them. All were of a remarkably gorgeous design, and the way they shone ruby-red in the evening sunlight, they looked more like newly constructed buildings than ruins.

"It has to be…over there…," Haruyuki muttered, continuing to stare intently at the cluster of temples he needed to burn into his memory.

It was the girls' school Kuroyukihime mentioned before they moved, the one that went from elementary all the way through university. In other words, the base of the White Legion, Oscillatory Universe.

Currently, of the six great Legions, that was the one they had the least connection with. Not only had he not fought them in the Territories, but he couldn't even remember having had a normal duel with any of its members. The only Linker from the Legion Haruyuki had seen was Ivory Tower, who attended the meeting of the Seven Kings as the White King's representative, and they didn't make much of an impression.

But the White Legion would almost certainly come to stand in the way of Kuroyukihime's fight for level ten. The White King, White Cosmos, was the one who had manipulated elementary school–age Kuroyukihime and caused the first Red King, Red Rider, to lose all his points, and Kuroyukihime viewed her as her ultimate enemy. The new Nega Nebulus—only just now at a total strength of seven people—was still a long way from standing shoulder to shoulder with the White Legion, but someday, the time for them to fight would come.

And when it does, I'm totally letting the White King have it. Deceiving your little sister, making her cry, getting her chased out of your house, is that what an older sister—what a parent—does?

His resolve hardened in his heart as Haruyuki burned Oscillatory Universe's headquarters into the back of his eyes.

When he whirled around, Takumu was just raising a hand from the north side of the tower. "Heeey! Haru! Time to get going!"

"Sorry. I'm coming!" By the time he ran over, his mind had switched gears, back to the Metatron mission.

5

Tokyo Midtown was a large, mixed-use facility that had opened for business exactly forty years earlier in 2007. The area was redeveloped after the Ministry of Defense moved to Ichigaya, with a total construction cost of about 370 billion yen. For a private enterprise, it was an unthinkably large project in the eyes of Japan of 2047 and its continually shrinking economy—or so said the article Haruyuki had found online. And as noted in that article, it was even at present one of the top landmarks in the city, alongside nearby Roppongi Hills (itself apparently costing a total of 270 billion yen).

Midtown Tower, the center of the facility, had a height of 248 meters. Of course, in the forty years since it opened, any number of taller buildings had been built all over Japan, but its majestic appearance, surfaces covered in mirrored glass, still had not lost its freshness. The lower levels were taken up by a bank, doctor's offices, meeting rooms, and the like, while the central floors were offices. And then the higher floors were occupied by a super-luxury hotel.

At the meeting of the Seven Kings on Sunday the week before, the destruction of the ISS kit main body had been the main agenda item. At that time, in addition to a head-on attack in which they charged the tower while avoiding Metatron's blows in the Unlimited Neutral Field, they had also examined the surprise move of first getting into Midtown Tower in the real world and *then* accelerating.

Penetrating the office floors was close to impossible, but you could go into the bank on the lower level with a free pass. But the problem was that there was no way to secure a safe place to dive into the Unlimited Neutral Field. With a normal duel, which only lasted at most 1.8 seconds, you could manage in the bank lobby, but you didn't know when a fight in the Unlimited Neutral Field would end. No one could predict how long it would take to move from the first floor to the highest levels and destroy the kit main body. Assuming it ended up being a long-term mission over several days, that would mean nearly ten children occupying a bench in the bank lobby on a full dive for five or ten minutes; there was no doubt that the security guard would come and stop them.

In the end, if they were going to go with the strategy of accelerating from within Midtown Tower in the real world, they would need to start by diving from the higher floors and quickly destroy the kit main body. But there, they ran into a fresh problem: the expensive luxury hotel that occupied the top floors.

Before the spread of Neurolinkers and social cameras, no matter how high-class the hotel, anyone could apparently breeze by the front desk and go up to the guest floors. But now with the concept of security greatly changed, gates were in place at pretty much every hotel that would not allow passage without Neurolinker authentication.

Thus, in order to set foot on the higher floors, they would need to be official guests of the hotel, but even the cheapest rooms started at the special fee of thirty thousand yen a night, and there was no one even at the meeting of the Seven Kings who could simply plop down a sum like that. Perhaps it would have been possible to raise enough for several people to stay there by collecting however much from the members of all the Legions, but the instant they did that, the Legions of the Accelerated World would sink to the level of a real-world outlaw group. Even if they did succeed in destroying the ISS kit main body, they would inevitably bring about an unwelcome change in the nature of the Accelerated World.

Given all these various circumstances, Haruyuki and his companions were simply walking northwest along a paved road made of cracked marble. To keep from drawing the attention of Enemies or other Burst Linkers with the noise from the engine, they weren't using Niko's tank either.

Niko herself was at the head of the group with Kuroyuki-hime, while Chiyuri and Takumu were discussing something as they walked alongside each other. Behind them was the parent-and-child team of Akira and Pard, but they didn't appear to be having any kind of conversation. Haruyuki was walking by himself a little ways off to the side, and Utai and Fuko, seated in her wheelchair, took up the rear.

Because the old Tokyo Tower and Tokyo Midtown were surprisingly close, with only 1.2 kilometers separating them, even at a slow walk it wouldn't take the group fifteen minutes to travel there. Several minutes from that moment, the biggest battle Haruyuki had ever been a part of would begin, but his heart was mysteriously silent.

"…what I had to do…" The words slipped out of him unawares, and apparently hearing this faint murmur, Aqua Current in front of him slowed down to come up beside him.

"You say something?"

"Huh? Um. Curren, you have good ears, huh…?"

"Water transmits sound almost four times better than air."

"I—I get it. It's no big deal. I was just telling myself that I did all the things I had to do for today's fight."

"Things you had to do…" Akira thought that over before saying distinctly, "I might still have something left."

"Huh…? You mean something you have to do?"

"Yes. Before we all accelerated, I went up to level four to enter the Unlimited Neutral Field, but I still haven't selected those level-up bonuses. And if I use the points I have left, I can go up more levels."

"Huh?!" Haruyuki cried out, but then he quickly understood. For over two years, Akira—Aqua Current—had fought in tag teams with low-level Linkers as the Accelerated World's lone bouncer. As a result, she had claimed successive victories to the point where she had been given the nickname The One, but in the process, she herself would have ended up earning the same number of points as her clients. The higher the opposing team's level, the more points you got when you won, so Akira had to have amassed a relatively large stash. Enough to be able to go up to level five or six, forget level four.

Compared with Pard, who immediately went up to level eight, Akira was indeed cautious in stopping at the four required to dive into the Unlimited Neutral Field. But...

"But that's just how it is," Haruyuki said. "When I was getting my level-up bonuses, too, I wrestled with it for a super-long time. And I mean, levels, you have to make it so you don't go up until you've got a fair bit of a safety margin, too. I think this thing you have to do is something you should take time to think about. Like, how do you want to grow your duel avatar—I mean, regrow it?"

Now Aqua Current blinked her pale-blue eye lenses as though surprised. But the expression soon left her face, and a hint of a gentle laugh bled onto her face mask through the film. "...I can't believe it was only eight months ago when I guarded you on the verge of total point loss."

"Huh? What do you mean?"

"I mean, you've grown. Proof that you've really done the things you needed to do. In the Accelerated World, and in the real world."

"Hayuh." A strange sound slipped out of Haruyuki, and he hurried to add, "I-it's just you yourself never feel that you've grown, you know? I definitely don't want any regrets in the two

missions today, so I was just thinking about whether there's anything left I need to do or think about while we walk."

"You were..." Akira hung her head, as though she were reflecting on herself. "I actually *do* have something still. Something to
do—no, say—before the mission."

His heart rose up in his throat for a second, but fortunately—he
supposed—Akira's gaze was turned not on Haruyuki to her left,
but on Pard walking up ahead. "Leopard."

Her name called, the leopard-headed avatar twitched her triangle ears before slackening her pace and arriving at Haruyuki's
left. Pinned between the two of them for some reason, Haruyuki
shrank into himself.

"Leopard—Myah," Akira began speaking to her scion over his
head. "I have to apologize to you."

"..."

The words were rather sudden, but apparently understanding
that this was not the whole of it, Pard said nothing in response.
Without the slightest visible reaction, she continued to walk
silently forward.

Akira also turned her gaze ahead and began to speak again
after a slight pause. "I'm sorry about that time. I was wrong."

Once again, Pard didn't make a move to reply. Her steps utterly
soundless, she stayed fifty centimeters to Haruyuki's left. Unable
to endure the increasingly strained atmosphere, Haruyuki was
about to quietly fall back when—

"NP," Pard murmured, and Haruyuki nearly let out a sigh
of relief. But the instant he heard the words that followed, the
virtual air got stuck in his throat. "...Or not. I was really angry.
Incredibly. Than I've ever been."

Given that the impatient alien Pard had always sought brevity
in her utterances and was now using three different emphasizers,
she must certainly have been, without exaggeration, seriously
angry. What on earth had Akira done to her "child" Pard?

As Haruyuki jerked his legs back and forth, his upper body

completely frozen, Akira turned to him and explained briefly, "A little while ago, I tried to erase Leopard's memory."

"What...?!" Haruyuki stumbled in his surprise, and Pard quickly grabbed his left arm to hold him up. But unable to take this in, Haruyuki simply stared at Akira. The flowing water that covered her face mask shuddered and her voice flowed out once more.

"Even after my avatar was sealed away at the Castle and I stopped dueling except for guarding, I still saw and talked with Leopard in the real sometimes. I wanted her to stop the freeze on leveling up. I might be her parent, but the members of Prominence couldn't have thought too highly about her ceasing to level for the sake of another Legion's member. Plus, someone might have tried a PK on her, eyes set on her vast sum of points. But no matter how many times I said it, Myah wouldn't listen." Akira let out a brief sigh, generating a few bubbles from the inside of her watery mask.

"You need a large sum of points to resist Seiryu's Level Drain," Pard said, nearly whispering, still holding Haruyuki's arm. "It was you, Aki, who taught me that. You."

"I've regretted telling you any number of times."

Here, their conversation stopped, and Haruyuki timidly asked, "...So then you tried to erase Pard's memories of Seiryu?"

"Not quite. My Memory Leak technique isn't as handy as all that. I explained a little before the Territories yesterday, but what I can erase is only *memories related to me.*"

"What?! ...S-so then what you tried to erase was...you, Curren...," Haruyuki babbled, dumbfounded, when suddenly, he felt an intense pressure in his left arm. He looked to see Pard squeezing the thin armor of his upper arm as hard as she could—although her claws had fortunately been tucked away. This sensation triggered a memory from a dozen or so hours earlier: the brief exchange between Blood Leopard and Aqua Current immediately after she made it back from Seiryu's altar alive.

—*I told you... You were supposed to forget me.*

—Can't forget your parent.

"You were…serious…," Haruyuki murmured.

Akira nodded slightly. "I tried to take her by surprise in her bedroom and have a direct duel. But when I was *this* close…"— she held finger and thumb about three centimeters apart—"…she got out of my pin."

In his heart, Haruyuki thought that only stood to reason. The real Akira Himi was probably in the same grade as Haruyuki, while Pard, whose real name he still didn't know (but was likely something close to Myah), was in grade ten, like Fuko. Adding in the height difference and that Pard must have had a fair bit of upper body strength, given the way she handled that large electric motorcycle, it would have been difficult to hold her down and force her to direct.

Put another way, Current had gone to those lengths to erase Pard from inside her. As a parent, to protect her child…

"It's not that I didn't understand how you felt, Aki," Pard said quietly, relaxing her grip on Haruyuki slightly. "The reason I was angry is because you thought you could make me forget you. No matter what you do, there's no way I'd forget. Not just in the real world, but in the Accelerated World, too, you're my precious…" She didn't say the words that came next, but rather slowly released Haruyuki's arm.

"I'm sorry," Akira apologized again. "I thought you'd end up in a sealed state, too, Myah. But I was wrong. And even with my avatar sealed away, I kept moving forward bit by bit. You were the same. Leveling up isn't the only way to get stronger. I should have known that better than anyone."

"That's right, Curren."

Surprised by this voice, Haruyuki looked up and saw Kuroyukihime, who had appeared right before him at some point. Advancing with a hovering motion, she had only her upper body turned back.

It wasn't just Kuroyukihime. He'd thought Chiyuri, Takumu, Fuko, and Utai were focused on their individual conversations ahead of and behind him, but all, and even Niko, were moving in a circle around Haruyuki, Akira, and Pard. Apparently, they all had been listening in.

Kuroyukihime turned to Akira. "I also cut myself off from the global net for two years and locked myself up in a tiny shell, but...recently, I've come to think that even that time was not wasted. The past and the present, and the future as well, they're connected. All the time that has passed creates 'now.' This 'now,' when I am walking here with you like this."

"And, like, Current." The Red King, who was walking nimbly beside the Black King, started to speak. "I mean, not thinking too much of Pard's level freeze, that wasn't it at all, y'know? Of course, no one but me knew the details or anything, but even still, they all understood. They were rooting for her. Like, Pard's fighting for some kid who's really important to her. And basically, I'm just saying here, but me and Pard fighting with Nega Nebulus like this in and of itself is a betrayal of the Legion if you're looking at it from outside. But I believe in them. Once this is all over and I explain what the what is, all thirty-two of Promi's members are gonna understand just fine." Done speaking, Niko whirled around again, but Akira still stayed silent for a while.

Abruptly, she looked up at the madder-red sky. The flowing water of her entire body shone with the reflection of the eternal evening sun.

"Precisely because there is the past, there is now..." Her voice was quiet, like the babbling of a small stream, but it sank deep into Haruyuki's mind and probably the minds of everyone else there. "The now is connected, and the future is born. Maybe because I gained the power to interfere just a little with the past, the now and the future receded from me. If I'd been able to accept the past, maybe I would have forgotten...that now is something that shines so brightly..."

At some point, they had all stopped, and the group now stood in the middle of the wide street, looking up at the sky.

Haruyuki couldn't help but see himself in Akira's words. For him, the past was hard and painful, a stratum of memory he'd like to forget if he could. No matter where he dug in it, the scenes unearthed only stabbed at his heart. But the truth was that any number of small, shining fragments were buried in there, too: Kuroyukihime appearing in the virtual squash corner of the Umesato Junior High local net. The children's park where he ran around playing with Chiyuri and Takumu, covered in mud. And the distant, distant memory of walking in the evening in Koenji, holding hands with his parents.

The Brain Burst program stretched out "now" a thousand-fold. Maybe it was escapist. A shelter to run to from painful reality where you could heal your wounds together with companions similarly suffering; maybe this was also one part of the nature of the Accelerated World. But that was certainly not all of it. This expanded "now" also included the past and the future. You could find precious gems in the past expanded by a thousand, and you could see the future that would come at some point, with a thousand times the clarity. That was this place, the Accelerated World.

"...Let's bring them together," Fuko murmured from behind him, her voice reminiscent of a slight spring breeze. "The past to the future. To that end...Let's fight now with all our might." She pointed a slender hand up to the northwest.

A massive silhouette there cut out a dark piece of the evening sky.

They'd come within a distance of five hundred meters already.

Midtown Tower: Round marble pillars stood lining the walls with stone statues—somehow divine, somehow eerie—adorning the capitals. Straining his eyes to peer at the upper part of the tower, he saw nothing, as usual—but he could definitely feel it. The presence of something lording over the world below from far up on high.

Unable to endure the heavy invisible pressure, Haruyuki started to step back.

And then like Fuko, Kuroyukihime raised her right hand, turning the sharp tip of her sword toward the peak of the tower.

The indomitable Niko clenched her small hand into a fist and thrust it up. Akira and Pard followed suit, and Utai and Chiyuri did the same soon after. Takumu brandished his Pile Driver, and finally, Haruyuki poured all the fighting spirit he could muster into his right hand and pointed it at the top of Midtown Tower.

This gesture naturally had no attack power. But Haruyuki could definitely see how the will released by their nine hands fused to become a beam that pierced the sky and reached the distant tower. And a massive silhouette casually twisting on the top of that tower.

"It seems our declaration of war has been received," Kuroyukihime announced boldly, slashing directly down with the sword of her right hand. When they all brought their hands down, the ebony avatar turned back and said, "Well then, let's confirm our strategy once more here. According to the information Haruyuki received from Iron Pound, Metatron's aggro range has a radius of two hundred meters. But if we inch right up to the edge of it and we end up attacked first, this will all be for naught, so our standby position is two hundred and fifty meters from the Tower."

Kuroyukihime bent forward and drew a small square with the tip of her sword in the white paving stone. She surrounded this with another large square.

"The small square is Midtown Tower, the big one is the Tokyo Midtown site. The northern half of the site is a park, and there are basically no obstacles up to the tower. Thus, our charge will be from the park in the north. First, Silver Crow will take the lead from the standby position and stop at the point where Metatron reacts. Two seconds later, the laser will be fired, so once we confirm that it can be defended with the Optical Conduction ability, you move forward and the rest of us will follow. I expect we'll reach the tower before a second shot is fired, but if we don't make it, Crow stops in the lead once more and deals with the laser. That is the basic plan."

This was the strategy he'd already heard on the roof of the old

Tokyo Tower, but Haruyuki was made aware all over again of the importance of the role he'd been given.

He would absolutely repel Metatron's laser. This resolve was unshakable, but what if…in the worst case, he managed to defend against the first shot of the laser but not the second? It wouldn't just be Haruyuki then; all his friends would also die instantly deep in Metatron's territory, and then be hit with the laser and die again after they regenerated. They might end up in Unlimited EK. Whatever else happened, he had to prevent that at least from happening. He *had* to.

"…Once you turn right at that intersection you can see there, you're at the park, our standby position. First, we'll check if there are any other Enemies in the area…"

Kuroyukihime continued giving instructions, and as he listened, Haruyuki stroked the metallic armor of his right arm with the tips of his fingers. A groove that hadn't been there before ran along it from wrist to elbow: It was a light-guiding rod that had appeared together with the awakening of his Optical Conduction ability. It hardly stood out at all compared with the silver wings on his back, but it was definitely there, proof of his new power.

Please. Protect everyone…and Rin, too, Haruyuki murmured to a small part of his heart, before clenching his hand into a resolute fist.

Approximately fifteen hours of inside time since their first dive…

The seven members of Nega Nebulus and the two from Prominence stood at the starting point for their final mission, the attack on Archangel Metatron. They stood at the edge of Midtown Garden, spreading out to the north of Tokyo Midtown.

With basically no buildings inside the park, there was only a smooth grassy field between them and the enormous tower soaring up into the sky two hundred and fifty meters ahead. All they had to do now was get into the agreed formation and move on the tower. Or so he thought.

"…Huh? What's that…?" Chiyuri muttered, baffled, the moment

the large park entered their field of view. The others also halted in front of the marble arch that was the entrance to the park.

On the north side of the grass, there was something strange about thirty meters from Metatron's attack range. An enormous, elliptical object. But it wasn't a perfect ellipse; the lower part grew heavily fatter, while the upper part looked like it narrowed in. It was perhaps six or seven meters tall with a circumference of about four meters.

"What the—? Doesn't look like an Enemy, though...," Niko said, narrowing her eye lenses. Scarlet Rain had an ability called Vision Extension, allowing her to "see" types of information that couldn't normally be seen. But Haruyuki could also tell that the elliptical body was no Enemy. Because no matter how many times he blinked, he saw no health gauge.

"An object that was originally in the park in the real world was re-created here...maybe?"

Haruyuki was about to agree with Takumu, but that opinion was rejected by Fuko.

"No, as far as I know, there's no object like that in this place. And if it was re-created in the Twilight stage, it should be white marble."

"True. This sphere—or rather, egg—how can we express the color of it? Sort of black, sort of green, sort of brown..."

Just as Kuroyukihime said, in the red evening sun, all that could be said was the elliptical body was a fairly concentrated color. But more than the color, Haruyuki felt like the word *egg* triggered something in his memory. Like he had seen something before in the Accelerated World and thought, *It's like an egg*. Or maybe he hadn't?

"Hey, Haru?" Chiyuri murmured quietly, having come up beside him. "I—I feel like I've seen something like this somewhere before."

"Huh? You too?"

"You mean, you do, too?"

They exchanged glances and then cocked their heads to the same side—and cried out briefly at the same time, "Oh!"

Unaware of the doubtful eyes of Kuroyukihime and the others turned their way, they stared once more at the blackish object.

He had actually seen something that looked very much like this. And only four days ago. In the Unlimited Neutral Field where he had dived with Chiyuri looking for a chance to obtain the Theoretical Mirror ability. And it hadn't been an object—a "thing." Nor an Enemy nor an Enhanced Armament. But a Burst Linker, just like Haruyuki and the others.

"B-but, Chiyu, he's…so big," Haruyuki babbled hoarsely.

And then.

A red light blossomed in the jet-black part of the massive elliptical body, where the evening sun didn't reach. Not a reflection of the western sun. A deeper, more concentrated red, the red of fresh blood. The light flickered two or three times. The instant he saw that biological movement, Haruyuki instinctively knew: The source of the light was an eye. An Enhanced Armament in the form of a crimson eyeball.

An ISS kit.

"That's…the enemy!" Haruyuki shouted in a trance, and everyone there braced themselves.

The elliptical body moved. It pulled itself up heavily, shuddering slowly, almost like a great beast awakening from a long slumber. The lower half of the black egg, sunk into the grass, hid short legs.

"Enemy?! An *Enemy*?!" Kuroyukihime cried, baffled.

"No!" Haruyuki hurriedly shook his head. "A Burst Linker!"

"B-but this size…"

Her skepticism was only natural. Now that it had stood up, the egg-shaped avatar was taller than the Red King with her Enhanced Armament fully deployed. And while the "he" Haruyuki had seen four days earlier had been enormous for a duel avatar, it hadn't been this aberrant size. Haruyuki didn't know why he had grown to three times that size or what he was doing here now, but it was a fact that he was an ISS kit user, and at the same time—

"He's Magenta Scissor's friend," Chiyuri finished Haruyuki's thought out loud, and the tension amongst their group immediately grew.

Takumu's reaction was particularly remarkable; inhaling sharply, he readied the pile driver of his right arm. "So then, a preemptive strike!"

"Wait, Taku!" Haruyuki hurried to stop Takumu, who was about to charge forward. "Physical effects totally don't work on this guy! His weak points, I'm pretty sure it's fire and, um..."

"Freeze plus strike!" Chiyuri—naturally—cried out, but there was none among the nine who could use ice. Instead, they had two Burst Linkers who were skilled with flame attacks.

"Let me at 'im!"

"Us!"

Niko and Utai sprang to the front and got into position. A crimson overlay enveloped Niko's fist, while a flame arrow burned brightly in Utai's long bow.

"If possible, aim for the ISS kit!" Kuroyukihime let a sharp command fly toward the two small yet reliable backs. "Be careful of Incarnate technique counterattacks! Fire!"

Hrrrn! The air shuddered, and fist and arrow of flame were launched. The attack was of such force that a midlevel Burst Linker or lower would have easily been sent flying. The egg avatar's movements were sluggish; it was already too late for it to defend or escape. The two flames ferociously closed in on the ISS kit stuck to the front of the torso.

Plark!

With a wet sound, the egg split in half. The enormous "mouth" that had tried to swallow up the master of the Legion Petit Paquet, Chocolat Puppeteer, four days earlier opened wide. There were no teeth or tongue to be seen inside; it was filled with a sticky darkness.

And from that darkness came five or six ink-black energy bullets. These collided with the flame bullets head-on and immediately began to swell up in the air. Haruyuki braced himself for an explosion that never came. Instead, the swirling crimson and ebony energy balls grew smaller before his eyes, as though perhaps their force canceled each other out.

In other words, given that the nihilistic something launched from the mouth of the egg avatar had canceled out even Niko's Radiant Beat, it was an Incarnate attack. Haruyuki only knew one type of long-distance technique like that: Dark Shot, one of the two techniques the ISS kit gave to users. But that could only be launched from the right or left hand.

"Why...from the mouth?!" Haruyuki let slip out, dumbfounded, and then, before his eyes, something even more surprising happened:

The mouth of the massive egg avatar opened to a height of two meters and a width of four, and one human shape after another jumped out. There were five, ten—more than that. The silhouettes, of various shapes and sizes, were nothing other than battle puppets.

"Rain! Maiden! Get back!"

At Kuroyukihime's command, the long-distance Niko and Utai withdrew. Haruyuki stepped forward with Takumu to protect them, but that was about as much as he could keep up with things.

He stared dumbfounded at the new Burst Linkers in front of the egg avatar. Once a thirteenth avatar had jumped up high into the air and done a somersault before landing on the grass, the egg finally closed its mouth. And then, almost as if it had thrown up everything inside it, the massive egg shrank before their eyes.

Once it reached the two-and-a-half-meter height, the contraction of the egg avatar stopped. But that was how Haruyuki knew it: The short limbs; the small, round eyes—it was without a doubt Avocado Avoider.

And the slender F-type avatar, standing with the group of Burst

Linkers thirteen strong lined up behind her, was none other than Magenta Scissor, the very Burst Linker Haruyuki and his friends had fought a fierce battle with four days earlier and who had parasitized Ash Roller with the ISS kit.

With a form that looked as though dark-reddish-purple bandages had been wound around her entire body, Magenta smiled sweetly, her mouth the only part of her entire body exposed. And perhaps as a way of offering a greeting, she opened the arms crossed in front of her chest, spreading them out to both sides. Along with this gesture, the bandage armor on her chest melted away to reveal the ISS kit attached there. The blood-red eyeball also shone somewhat darkly on the bodies of all the avatars behind her, including Avocado.

Ten meters apart, Magenta's crew of thirteen and the nine in Haruyuki's group faced one another. A low murmur broke the tense silence.

"How...did...?" The owner of the voice was Takumu, still carefully wielding the Enhanced Armament of his right arm at the ready.

Haruyuki finished the sentence in his mind. *How on earth did you ambush nine people?*

Magenta was the one who attacked Ash Roller the previous day, so she might have anticipated that Haruyuki and his friends would go so far as to take on the challenge of destroying the ISS kit main body today in order to save Ash. But it would have been absolutely impossible to specify a precise time. And this was the Unlimited Neutral Field, where time was accelerated by a factor of a thousand. Even if they had been lying in wait since ten o'clock that morning real time, a simple calculation showed that more than three months would have passed on the inside.

If you waited in one place, alert to your surroundings, for that length of time, when your target did eventually show up, you would have been totally exhausted and unable to fight. In other words, an ambush in the Unlimited Neutral Field was, in practical terms, impossible. The only one who could pull it off was the

lone—as far as Haruyuki knew—Burst Linker with the ability to decelerate, the vice president of the Acceleration Research Society, Black Vise.

So he's pulling strings again? The thought flashed through Haruyuki's mind. When it came to Black Vise, it *was* possible that he'd been hiding around Midtown Tower since the morning, and then when he discovered his target, he could have returned to the real world to inform Magenta and her gang. But in that case, considering the time lag on the real side, Magenta and the others would have had to show up after Haruyuki and his friends. So that theory was contradicted by the fact that Avocado Avoider had been there when they arrived at the park. And Black Vise and his Acceleration Research Society likely thought Metatron alone was enough to guard Midtown Tower, so Haruyuki couldn't believe he would expend such effort on Magenta's behalf when she wasn't even a comrade.

Haruyuki had thought this much through while he inhaled and exhaled, but he still absolutely could not understand how Magenta had managed to succeed in an ambush. As he racked his brain while he got into a fighting stance, Magenta smiled thinly and finally spoke.

"Hello, Silver Crow. It's been a while, Cyan Pile. I'm glad we could meet again."

"...I actually never wanted to see you again," Takumu responded in a hard voice. He had come across Magenta in the Setagaya area in the middle of the month and been given a sealed ISS kit card. He had obtained it at first for the sake of gathering information, but pushed into an unavoidable situation, Takumu had equipped it and very nearly been dragged down into the dark side of Incarnate.

Glossy lips still stretched out in a grin, Magenta shrugged her sharp shoulders lightly. "So cold! I was ever so looking forward to our reunion, y'know?"

"Then prove it. Tell me how you managed to ambush us,"

Takumu demanded, not entirely sure about where the "prove it" part of his statement was going to go.

"Sure thing." Magenta's smile turned wry, but she agreed readily. "I had to make my apologies for breaking my promise with Crow and all."

"Promise...?" Haruyuki parroted, before finally remembering. When they fought in the Setagaya Area four days earlier, he had indeed exchanged words like a promise with Magenta: *"Are you going to achieve your goal first, or will we destroy the ISS kit main body first?"* The woman had come that day to block Haruyuki and his friends from destroying the kit main body, so that couldn't have been construed as him breaking that promise. But then, what on earth was Magenta ultimately doing?

As he listened with half an ear to Chiyuri explaining the situation to Kuroyukihime and the others behind him, Haruyuki tossed out the question inside him. "But, Magenta, if you hadn't forcefully parasitized Ash Roller with an ISS kit yesterday, we wouldn't have hurried like this to destroy the kit main body. Why? Why did you target Ash?!"

"Can't answer that, sadly. Got obligations of my own...But your first question. The answer's simple. The hard part of an ambush in the Unlimited Neutral Field is you can't handle the passing time. I mean, the days, the months, right? But what if you didn't feel time? You could wait however long you wanted then, right?"

"Didn't feel...time?"

Time was indeed extremely subjective. Fun times passed quickly, while hard times flowed slowly. But there was no way an ambush was fun. Time you spent standing by on guard for an enemy who might appear anywhere at any time would actually feel longer, wouldn't it? The words meant as a hint only deepened his doubts.

"I see." A quiet voice came from behind him. "So there's a secret to the egg-shaped duel avatar behind you then? You didn't get in his mouth just to hide yourselves?"

"Sooo insightful. But he's not an egg, he's an avocado. He's not so great at talking, so I'll do the introductions. This is Avocado Avoider. A pleasure."

Perhaps because his name was called, the dark-green avatar parked at the very rear stirred slightly. He had gotten a fair bit smaller, but even still, he was without a doubt the largest of the twenty-three avatars there.

Magenta Scissor brought her right hand down to her hip. "*Avoider* means someone who avoids, but that's not all. Originally, the word meant *to void*, y'know."

"To…void?"

"Yup. There's nothing but a void inside Avocado's mouth. And 'cause there's no space, he can get any number of people in there. *And there's no time, so when you're in there, you don't feel outside time.* Although once he swallows you, your avatar gradually melts into the void, so you need some defenses against that."

Haruyuki needed two seconds or so to comprehend what Magenta Scissor was saying. The instant he managed to imagine it somehow, he cried out in surprise. "What?! So then, you mean, it's like this? When you go into Avocado's mouth in the Unlimited Neutral Field, and then his mouth opens again right away and you get out, a serious amount of time has actually passed. Something like that?"

"That's exactly it, Crow. From my perspective, I only jumped into Avocado's mouth a second ago. Incidentally, we started this ambush here at a little before nine in real-world time. What time's it now, hmm?"

"…About twelve thirty."

"Three hours, hmm? Which means that nearly five months have passed over here, huh? Normally, we'd have gotten sick of waiting and lost even the energy to talk, but this is how it is, so you don't need to worry." Magenta Scissor grinned.

"Yer a damned liar, Magenta Scissor, or whoever you are." A low voice containing a fierce heat came flying at her.

It was Niko. When Haruyuki glanced back, the Red King stood next to the Black King, glaring at Magenta Scissor, a sharp light shining in her large eye lenses.

"Oh my! *Liar?* Whatever do you mean?"

"Don't play dumb. You know what I'm talking about. I don't know anything about this void or whatever of yours, but it's true thirteen of you went into Avocado Avoider's mouth and didn't feel time. But, you know, what about Avocado? He didn't wait here in this park all sharp and focused by himself for five months, now, did he? You hafta know how hard that would be."

Following the shower of verbal attacks—a rain of high-temperature flames—the smile finally faded from Magenta Scissor's mouth and disappeared.

But it wasn't Magenta Scissor who responded to Niko, but rather Avocado himself standing at the rear.

"I'm...fine...!" Avocado shouted, tiny round eyes blinking. "I. Was asleep. The whole time...! So. I'm fine...!"

He was parasitized by the ISS kit beneath his large mouth, but somehow, Avocado appeared to have maintained his self, although not to the extent Magenta Scissor had. In contrast, the twelve lined up in front of him were uniformly silent, the light gone from their eye lenses. When Haruyuki thought back, Avocado had repeated "Like. Chocolat," while he was trying to eat Chocolat Puppeteer four days earlier.

The large avatar was about to shout something more, and Magenta Scissor stopped him with a hand. Turning to Niko, she bowed lightly.

"It's a pleasure to meet you, Red King. I didn't expect you and Bloody Kitty to be involved, but I am very glad to see you...Just as you say, I did push Avocado into a difficult role. I at least should have kept him company during the overly long wait, but I didn't. But that's not to say that waiting would have been annoying...If I was going to take on the Black King, then I wanted to fight in perfect condition. That's all."

Hearing this, Kuroyukihime responded in a voice like a honed blade, "So the sealed ISS kit card you gave Crow was indeed a challenge to me then, Magenta Scissor."

"Well, it did end up being that. Although it's quite a bit sooner than I'd planned. But to wish for any more than this would be greedy. Because my full battle power is set up here now, on this most perfect stage, where not only can no one interfere, but there is no time limit. If it means I can have an all-out war with the Black King, then I will be content to accept any censure."

"...I believe this is our first meeting. Why are you so eager to fight me?"

Magenta didn't reply to Kuroyukihime's question right away. She moved her long, slender fingers to stroke the single short sword equipped on each hip. Beneath the bandage armor that covered the majority of her face, her lips tightened firmly for an instant. When she spoke eventually, it was the sharpest and coldest Haruyuki had ever head Magenta Scissor sound. "That is because you were born with something very big, Black Lotus."

"Oh? And what might that be?"

"You actually got too many big things to count, but...To sum them all up, I suppose it would be power and will? When you dropped down into the Accelerated World as a Burst Linker, you already had overwhelming battle power and an unshakeable will. That form of yours is proof of that."

Magenta raised her right hand without a sound and thrust her index finger at Kuroyukihime.

"The general principle of same level, same potential? Heh-heh, that makes me laugh. Everyone actually knows it, deep down. Some Burst Linkers are strong and some are not, right from the start."

You can't just say that! Haruyuki wanted to shout. The word *potential* didn't only refer to abilities and special attacks. Even if you had hardly any special attacks or Enhanced Armament when you landed in the Accelerated World, as long as you believed in the avatar your heart had produced and you continually reached your hand out to the sky, never giving up, your duel avatar would respond someday. Haruyuki had fought to that very day supported by this conviction.

But at the same time, the words Magenta had said to him four days earlier replayed in his ears. Avocado Avoider was abandoned by his parent immediately after being born and had his initial points stolen by Legion members, one of whom was his parent. On the brink of total loss, Magenta Scissor had given him an ISS kit, and he turned the tables to drive them to total loss instead.

There hadn't been a "someday" for Avocado. If Magenta hadn't intervened, he would definitely have had all his points stolen and been permanently exiled from the Accelerated World. Simply because he didn't have a powerful ability or a cool appearance. What saved Avocado hadn't been the principle of "same level, same potential," but rather the ISS kit.

Haruyuki gritted his teeth, unable to say anything, while Kuroyukihime stepped forward between him and Takumu.

"I will bear in mind your assertion. But what does that have to do with my form?"

This curt response brought a thin smile back to Magenta Scissor's lips. "...A duel avatar is born in the forge of mental trauma. Everyone knows that. If the shape and size of that trauma—that 'lack'—is reflected in the avatar...This is just my personal opinion, but the greater the symmetry of the avatar, the less that Burst Linker needs other people."

"Symmetry...? You mean, left and right have the same shape?"

"Yes. Left and right, front and back, top and bottom. When you really poke into symmetry, you see it's eternal. It's that perfect. You learned this in school, didn't you? Molecules with higher symmetry are more stable, they're not broken or bonded."

Had he learned something like that? Even in a situation like this, Haruyuki grew slightly uneasy and suddenly asked Pard, standing behind him to the left, "I-is that true?"

And her answer was: "Once the fight is over, look up *benzene* and *resonance stabilization*."

At any rate, these weren't the sort of terms you learned in eighth grade, so he nodded with an "O-okay" and turned to face forward again.

Kuroyukihime sloughed off a small shrug. "I think it's a bit of a stretch to force molecular symmetry onto a duel avatar. And if you're saying that my avatar has bilateral symmetry, then isn't it the same for you and your companions?"

"At a glance, maybe, sure. But, you see, Black King, that form of yours hides something almost no other avatar has, a perfect symmetry." Sounding mysterious, Magenta brought up her right hand in a supple motion and spread out her thin fingers.

Unable to immediately understand the meaning of the gesture, Haruyuki stared at Magenta Scissor's hand. It had the same five fingers as Haruyuki's—and pretty much every other duel avatar. The placement was also normal, and he couldn't see anything she would go out of her way to show them.

And then he finally understood.

When you looked at it like that, the hand of a duel avatar—no, a human being—didn't have bilateral symmetry. The lengths of the index finger and the pinkie finger were totally different, and there was nothing opposite the thumb. But only one person there in that place, only the Black Lotus alone, had hands that were symmetrical both side to side and front to back. As the blades of swords that cut through everything they touched.

Kuroyukihime likely understood what Magenta Scissor was trying to say the moment she raised her hand. But the Black King maintained her silence, while Magenta Scissor gazed at her squarely and continued in an even sharper voice, "Our hands are asymmetrical. Only when they are joined with someone else's do they become symmetrical. But, Black Lotus, your hands are different. Your two swords have just that, a perfect symmetry. You don't need anyone else. Because right from the start, you were born with everything you needed."

"Y-you can't just—!" Haruyuki cried wildly, unable to stand it anymore. "You can't know all that just from the way an avatar looks! And you! You said before you hate pairs! You're totally contradicting yourself now!"

"Oh my, that's a little off the mark, boyo." Magenta Scissor twirled her hand in the air. "What I hate is two being one. And I don't want to fight the Black King because she is the manifestation of ultimate symmetry. I hate that she went and made a child, formed a Legion, and plays around at being a parent or a friend or whatever when she has the strength to go however far she wants all by herself. Above all else, I simply can't swallow the Black Legion, the way you're all 'chosen knights to fight evil.'"

Her tone was subdued, but there were thick blades hiding in her words. In his rage, Haruyuki felt the world grow pale before his eyes. And Takumu and Chiyuri—and not just them, but Fuko and the others who had stayed silent so far—all radiated an aura like a colorless fire.

But even with this thrown at her, Kuroyukihime remained coolly dispassionate. "I see. I can finally understand what it is you're trying to say, Magenta Scissor. For you, and your goal of making the Accelerated World homogenous through the ISS kits, the so-called elite groups are your greatest enemy. But, well. This thing, the ISS kit, to begin with, it exists to create—" She cut herself off and shook her head lightly.

The words Kuroyukihime had swallowed were likely something along the lines of "To create the ultimate berserker." *The ISS kit main body accumulates a vast amount of negative will, all of that is poured into a high-level Enhanced Armament, and the Armor of Catastrophe Mark II is born.* —This was the theory Aqua Current had revealed three days earlier at the Arita house. It did seem like the sort of thing the Acceleration Research Society would think up, but unfortunately, they had no proof. Even if Kuroyukihime said it out loud now, it seemed unlikely she would be able to convince Magenta.

"...No," Kuroyukihime continued nonchalantly. "I shouldn't say anything about the kit at this late stage. Because we've come here to destroy it. And while I might accept your manner of speaking, the way you're treating us as an elite group...Given the situation, there's nothing I can say to change your mind on that matter. We'll tell the rest with our fists. And let you know whether or not our strength is simply what was given to us by the system." The Black King's tone concealed a steely core, the strength of iron polished to a shine.

"Right." Magenta accepted this squarely. "I've gotten to say basically everything I wanted to...But one final thing: If you win this fight, I don't care what you do with the fourteen of us. I wouldn't say nothing if you killed us repeatedly and forced us to total loss, even. But if we win...Black King, don't interfere with the ISS kits anymore. Promise to simply watch as the world is reborn."

"...You managed to succeed in a such difficult ambush, and yet, that's all you ask? If you win in the Unlimited Neutral Field, I think it would be more than possible to force total loss on us all or forcefully equip each of us with ISS kits."

"I'm good. As long as you have the Watch Witch, the kits'll be yanked off. And I can't even imagine how long it would take to send two kings to total loss. And...I want you all to see it. A world where the abilities of all avatars equalized, where there's no meaning in tag teams or Legions. A place where Burst Linkers who weren't born blessed in power or form will not be rejected for that reason. A new Accelerated World!"

The instant Magenta finished this fervent declaration, the eye lenses of the duel avatars lined up neatly behind her shone red all at once. Almost as if they were in powerful resonance with Magenta Scissor's overly radical thinking.

Most likely, the thirteen subordinates under Magenta, including Avocado, were Burst Linkers from the Setagaya and Ota areas. Like the two members of the Legion Petit Paquet, some had likely been forcefully parasitized with the kits against their will. But over two weeks had passed since the appearance of the kits, and now, with the synchronization every night through parallel processing, all these Burst Linkers had to be seen as having become one under Magenta Scissor's impressive conviction. Reaching out to individuals would no longer work.

"...Agreed. If we lose here, Nega Nebulus promises not to interfere until your objective is achieved. Although, even if every Burst Linker besides us ends up an ISS kit user, we have no intention of giving up the fight."

Magenta Scissor smiled with satisfaction at Kuroyukihime's declaration. "And *that* is why you're the Black King, hmm? All right then. How about we get started already? Sorry, but I'm not doing any tournament-style thing where we send out one representative at a time or any garbage like that. I have no interest in playing at war like that."

"Naturally, that wasn't what I was thinking, either. As long as you all are using the ISS kits—negative Incarnate techniques— then this is necessarily nothing other than a slaughter where rules do not apply. Also, whoever wins, you will learn. The terror, the brutality, and the futility of an Incarnate war in which everything is possible...The reason the Incarnate System has been kept hidden for so very long." Kuroyukihime's voice was actually quiet to the end, even sad. But at the same time, a faint bluish-purple shimmering overlay enveloped the ebony avatar, showing her firm will to fight.

The Black King angled back slightly and murmured to the group around her. "Rain, Raker, everyone. I know I said that to Magenta, but powerful Incarnate techniques will draw in large Enemies. So hold back in the opening stages, and then annihilate them all at once when I say go. Up against Burst Linkers, victory might be *slightly more attractive* to you...but we'll deal with that once everything is over."

"Yup," Niko said.

"Roger," Fuko responded, and the others nodded.

"Master," Takumu said, his voice concealing a strong resolve as he dropped into battle stance. "Will you leave Magenta Scissor to me at first? I was the one who created the connection between her and Nega Nebulus, after all."

"…I suppose. But don't stick out too much. I don't think anyone has forgotten, but this spot is just on the edge of Metatron's attack range. If we get too close to the tower, we'll be hit from above by the laser. The limit line is…" As she spoke, Kuroyuki-hime indicated with her eyes a marble path that cut across the grass east-west about twenty meters from the two-hundred-meter line that was Metatron's aggro range. "Let's set it at that path. No matter what happens, be careful you don't cross it."

Once again, they all nodded.

Ten meters to the south, Magenta, having similarly given instructions to her comrades, turned to face them again and removed the small swords equipped on either hip.

"Pile, I'm pretty sure you remember, but…," Haruyuki murmured.

"When those swords fuse, they become scissors, right?" Takumu was quick to respond. "It's okay. I'm thinking of countermeasures. Crow, you…Bell…"

"Leave it to me." Now it was Haruyuki assenting immediately. "I'll make sure to keep her safe."

This was normally when Chiyuri would fume at being treated like a child again, but this time, unsurprisingly, she moved behind Haruyuki without a word. She was probably the only one in this battle who couldn't use the Incarnate System. Haruyuki would have to protect their precious healer against any Incarnate techniques.

The eight led by the Black King and the thirteen under Magenta Scissor dropped into fighting stances all at the same time. *Kashak!* The dry air of the Twilight stage rapidly grew strained. The tension was so great, sparks threatened to electrify his metallic armor, and Haruyuki had a fleeting thought in one corner of his mind.

If this had been a normal group fight, this was the moment when he would have been carefully scanning each member of the enemy team before the fighting started, guessing at their abilities from the avatar color and shape. But there was basically no point in that in this battle—because all the Enemies besides Magenta would come at them with nothing but Dark Shot and Dark Blow, the Incarnate techniques from the ISS kit. The thirteen before him were all sizes, shapes, and armor colors, but that no longer indicated the Burst Linker's idiosyncrasies.

...*Magenta Scissor. Is that really the Accelerated World you want?*

Almost as if this question rattling around Haruyuki's mind ignited the highly compressed air of the battlefield, twenty-three duel avatars all leapt into motion.

6

Magenta's army made the first move.

Lined up in a row, twelve soldiers thrust out their right hands in perfect sync, with Avocado Avoider on the end taking on the same position a second later. The eye-shaped Enhanced Armament attached to their chests emitted flashes of muddy blood-red light.

""""Dark Shot.""""

The technique name was shouted with one voice—although this time, again, Avocado was a little behind—but had an ear-splitting dissonance. A dull-black aura swirled in thirteen palms, concentrated, and jetted forward in an ebony beam. *Zzzshm!*

In fights over the last two weeks, Haruyuki had seen and been on the receiving end of this technique any number of times, but this was the first time he'd been showered by this kind of concentrated attack. The nonmaterial bullets of nihilistic energy, containing enough power to potentially cause instant death with even one direct hit, came together in groups of four or five in midair and formed three lances charging toward them.

The first to react was Fuko, who had taken up position in the center of the Lotus army of nine.

"Swirl Sway!" Still seated in her wheelchair, she held her right hand in front of her to produce a green whirlwind. The wind that stretched out between Haruyuki and Kuroyukihime swelled in scope into something akin to a sideways tornado and essentially covered all nine as they stood firm.

The three large lances howled as they made contact with the tornado. *Heeeeeng!* They were sucked into the whirling wind, muddying the green spirals with black.

When they had fought Ash Roller's motorcycle, which was under the control of an ISS kit, in the middle of the school festival, Fuko had repelled two simultaneous dark shots with this technique. But now she was facing over six times that force. The hand supporting the tornado shook, and a faint pant slipped out from between her lips.

One of the lances was ejected from the tornado, an enormous spring bouncing backward, and plunged into a building behind them off to the right, gouging a large hole out of it. Another shot straight up into the air and disappeared in the twilight sky.

But the final lance fought against the centrifugal force like a living creature and inched its way to the source of the tornado. If the wriggling energy made it straight through, Fuko's entire arm would be sent flying. Unconsciously, Haruyuki stretched out the five fingers of his right hand so he could be ready with his Laser Sword. But if he wasn't careful, he would cut into the rotational force of the tornado and potentially set the wind free.

The ebony lance pulled forward bit by bit.

"*Maelstrom,*" a quiet voice said. Akira Himi—Aqua Current— produced a blue vortex in her outstretched left hand. It was very much like Fuko's technique, except rather than wind forming the tornado, it was water. Each of the scattering water droplets shone a pale blue, as proof of the technique's origins in the Incarnate System.

The blue approached the green tornado from the right, touched it, and instantaneously merged with it.

Krr! An incredible storm swelled up, and Haruyuki reflexively threw back his head. A myriad of water droplets spun out of the tornado, now doubled in size, to rain down on the surface of his armor and bounce off again. No doubt, if he happened to swallow one, the raindrop could probably have taken out a pretty good chunk of his health gauge.

With the added force of the waterspout, the tornado now had the power of a swirling current, and it thrust the black lance out, turning it 180 degrees before releasing it into the sky. Whistling through the air, the fused Dark Shot didn't make a direct hit on Magenta's army, but it did plunge into the grass nearby to send a black pillar of flames skyward, throwing the enemy off-balance.

"Now!" Kuroyukihime cried sharply. "Pile, Leopard! Charge with me! Rain, Maiden! Cover us! Raker, Current, you're defense. Bell, healing. Crow, protect Bell! Let's go!!"

"Okay!"

"K."

Takumu and Pard charged toward the enemy encampment alongside Kuroyukihime. Niko readied her handgun, Peace Maker, and Utai her longbow, Flame Caller, while Fuko and Akira prepared to defend against the next Dark Shot. And Haruyuki—well, at any rate, he looked at Chiyuri.

"H-heh-heh-heh…" The yellow-green witch-shaped avatar inclined her pointed hat. "Crow, thanks for the guard."

"Yeah, leave it to me!" he shouted, but to be honest, he could hardly stand still. Although he understood the importance of protecting their healer, an advantage their enemy didn't have, it was still frustrating not to be able to charge into battle with his leader.

"…Crow, maybe I should practice the Incarnate System, too," Chiyuri offered quietly, as though reading Haruyuki's mind. Her eyes were still on the front line.

"Huh…?" Instantly, his restlessness quieted. Readying himself for the next attack wave, he shook his head quickly. "No, you don't need to hurry. The truth is, it's better if you can get through without using it. Thanks to the ISS kits, we're attacked with Incarnate a lot more these days, but once we smash the main body, things should quiet down again. And then you can really think about it, no pressure."

"You really have grown, hmm, Corvus?" Fuko, rather than Chiyuri, responded to Haruyuki's murmured assurance.

"Huh?! No, it's just, I mean..."

"Once this is over and we go back to the other side, I will spoil you so hard. So right now, you make sure you do your job." Apparently, she too had seen right through to his desire to leap onto the battlefield.

Haruyuki tucked his head in and shouted, "Right!"

"Yaaaaaah!" Takumu's battle cry rang out over the enemy camp. "Cyan Blade!!"

It had been a while since Haruyuki had heard that technique name. The pile driver equipped in Cyan Pile's right arm emitted a flash of bright light and broke apart. Gripped in his left hand, only the spike remained, and it quickly transformed into a large two-handed sword. As a reminder that the sword was Incarnate, an overlay like blue flames snaked around the blade.

Adjusting his grip on the sword, Takumu yanked it up, readying it at waist height, while in front of him, Magenta Scissor crossed the small swords she held in each hand. *Ka-ching!* The two swords came together to form a pair of enormous scissors. And unlike when Haruyuki had fought her, the scissors themselves were enveloped in a dark aura.

"Be careful, Taku...!" Haruyuki couldn't help muttering, even though he knew he was too far away for his friend to hear him.

Magenta's scissors were equipped with an ability called Remote Cut. Each time the blades came together, an unseen severing force cut into a distant target. The only way to avoid the invisible attack was to leap far away from the invisible line extending outward from the tip of the scissors. But it was nearly impossible to keep that up when they were snipped open and closed in quick succession.

Unable to come up with a strategy for countering the long-distance cutting on his own, Haruyuki had enlisted the help of

Chocolat Puppeteer's Chocopet puppets, leaving him room to charge Magenta. But Chocolat wasn't there now. And Kuroyuki-hime and Pard were occupied with several ISS kit users, so they wouldn't be able to cover Takumu. Niko and Utai launched one flame bullet/arrow after another, but over half were met with Dark Blow, so the enemy wasn't exactly dropping like flies.

"Bell, when I give the order, please heal Pile."

"Roger." Chiyuri nodded.

Wheen! Magenta's scissors flashed through their dark aura, opening and closing at a ferocious speed, perhaps as much as five times a second. An unbroken chain of metallic shrieks joined orange sparks crackling around Takumu.

Haruyuki reflexively started to give the heal order, but forced himself to swallow it. When he looked very closely, he saw the Incarnate sword was doubling here as a shield to repel the majority of the cutting power. As she opened and closed the scissors, Magenta moved them up and down and side to side, but Takumu correctly traced the tip with his sword, avoiding a direct hit to his avatar.

But the situation could only get worse. Because Magenta's scissors were not a gun, in theory, she could continue to attack without end. On the other hand, Takumu couldn't keep dodging for the rest of time; he'd need to switch into a counterattack at some point, but he didn't have an opening to swing his sword. If he moved the blade from the line of sight for even a second, he might end up with his head chopped off.

I can create an opening with my Laser Lance. The thought flashed through his mind, but Haruyuki brushed it away. An enemy might target Chiyuri while he was launching his Incarnate technique. And more importantly, Takumu wanted to face off against Magenta himself, knowing full well the terror of Remote Cut. So then, he had to have a plan for turning this defense into an offense.

"…!" Haruyuki caught a glimpse of a black aura concentrating in the corner of his eye and readied both hands. "Dark Shot's coming!"

Simultaneously, the six on the enemy's right flank shot jet-black beams through the sky toward them. Rather than fusing together, however, the attacks this time were all whizzing toward different targets.

Fuko and Akira quickly held up their hands to generate the green-and-blue tornados that would defend themselves, Niko, and Utai from the Incarnate bullets aimed at them. Haruyuki also brought a silver overlay up into his hands and stared hard at the balls of darkness flying toward him and Chiyuri.

"Laser…" The sword of his right hand knocked the first shot out into the sky.

"…Sword!!" He hit the second shot with the sword of his left hand.

Having fulfilled his duty, Haruyuki turned his eyes back to the battle between Magenta and Takumu and unconsciously stiffened. The aura enveloping Takumu's Cyan Blade was flickering and looked to be on the verge of disappearing. Haruyuki could see countless scars running along the large blade. If this kept up, it would shatter.

When he thought about it, Takumu was essentially sacrificing his sword to defend against the nonphysical cutting power of Magenta's scissors, so it made sense that the damage that power did would accumulate in the sword alone. The grand premise of Brain Burst—no, of all fighting games—was that you couldn't win if you only defended, but this was exactly the situation Magenta's scissors were forcing Takumu into, making it a weapon far more fearsome than Haruyuki had thought.

Pleek! A remarkably large chunk of the blade broke off and fell to the ground.

Magenta Scissor grinned, and, fixing the direction of the scissors, opened and closed them with even more ferocity. She'd given up on targeting the main body of the avatar and was now trying to destroy the sword first. Sparks flickered and scatted like the sword was being held to a grinder, and the center of the two-handed blade grew visibly scarred.

It's going to break! Haruyuki gritted his teeth.

A cloud of dirt exploded upward at Takumu's feet. The massive blue body charged forward impossibly fast for such a large avatar. Repelling the invisible blades with the battered sword, he closed the distance from Magenta to five meters in an instant.

Whakeeen! The opening and closing of the scissors stopped.

Takumu's sword was jammed in between the two blades.

Here, Haruyuki finally understood Takumu's strategy. He had been intently waiting for the moment Magenta started to target his sword. As long as her sights were fixed, he could close the distance between them by simply charging forward. And then, if he could get the real scissors to bite down on his sword, Remote Cut could no longer be activated. Of course, Takumu could no longer move his sword either, but being a kendo practitioner, he knew ways to continue an attack when locked sword to sword.

"Ngh…Aaah!" With a roar, Takumu took another step in. Both hands, still gripping the hilt, slid under the scissors and slammed hard into Magenta's chest—into the crimson eyeball parasitizing her there.

He didn't quite smash it, but taking a blow with the full weight of a heavyweight avatar behind it, the ISS kit closed its upper and lower lids tightly, shooting dull-black sparks. Perhaps some of the damage splashed back onto Magenta herself; the body covered in reddish-purple bandages shuddered and reeled back. The hands gripping the scissors relaxed slightly, and not letting the moment slip away, Takumu pushed his sword up with all his might.

The large scissors, the origin of Magenta's name, flew out of their owner's hands and danced high into the sky. Takumu swung his sword into the overhead position for the first time in this fight and let out a loud battle cry.

"Eeeaaaaah!!" The dizzyingly fast slash attack overtook the falling scissors from above, cutting the lethal black weapon in two right in the middle. The separated blades shattered into countless fragments and scattered in all directions.

Taku! You did it! Haruyuki yelled in his mind.

The mental strength to keep the Incarnate sword materialized when it—and he—were so battered. The fortitude to wait
and watch for the chance to turn it all around in a unilaterally
defensive battle. And then, the explosive power to turn the tide
in an apparent deadlock. Haruyuki felt Takumu was more powerful than he was in all these ways, but his joy was much greater
than his frustration. Even as he kept his guard up and his eyes on
the enemy camp, he started to do a tiny fist pump on his friend's
behalf.

"Watch out!!" Chiyuri cried from behind him.

For a moment, he thought an enemy he had overlooked was
about to send a Dark Shot their way, but that wasn't it. Chiyuri
was calling out to Takumu. Magenta Scissor had fallen faceup in
front of him, seemingly still stunned from the direct hit to her
ISS kit, but her right hand held a black aura.

Takumu also noticed the dark swirling mass and tried to yank
his sword up again. But he was the slightest bit too late. An ebony
beam jetted out of Magenta's hand without any advance notice.

"Ngh...!" Takumu abandoned his attack and tried to defend
against the beam with his sword. Although he somehow managed to deflect its trajectory, the nihilistic stream grazed the side
of his helmet, scattering particles that resembled fresh blood.

But what was more serious was the damage to Cyan Blade.
Defending against the Dark Shot from extreme close range had
caused yet another large chunk to fall off, and the overlay was
disappearing. Takumu gave up on a counterattack and leapt
back.

Magenta stood up and took aim at Pile with her right hand as
she protected the eye on her chest with her left.

"She...Without the technique name, a Dark Shot..." Haruyuki groaned. In the battle four days earlier, Magenta Scissor
had needed to shout the name of the Incarnate technique to activate it. Which meant she had also evolved her abilities in this
short time. While he was impressed on the one hand, Haruyuki
couldn't stop himself from muttering. "...Why, though...?"

Why, when she had such ambition—the passion to set her sights ever higher—why would she devote it to the spread of the ISS kits? Why was she so driven that she would sacrifice even herself to realize a world in which all duel avatars had the same techniques, in which individuality lost all meaning?

Facing off against Takumu as she was, Magenta naturally couldn't answer Haruyuki's questions. Instead, she moved her left hand quickly, gesturing instructions to her comrades. The seven that Black Lotus and Blood Leopard had engaged in combat after breaking through enemy lines, and the six waging long-range war with Haruyuki's group all moved to the east side of the park, coming together in a tight formation. Magenta pulled back from Takumu to join them.

Neatly lined up in a double horizontal formation, with the back row centered on Avocado and the front on Magenta, the ISS kits radiated such enormous force that it was like the Burst Linkers had come together to make one super-massive duel avatar.

But when Haruyuki turned his gaze on each of the individual avatars, he saw Magenta was the only one uninjured. The other thirteen had taken damage all over from Kuroyukihime's swords, Pard's teeth and claws, Niko's gun, and Utai's flame arrows. And because Avocado had defended against Niko and Utai's long-range attacks with his body, his soft armor was riddled with bullet holes and burns.

Rather than pursuing the collected enemy army, Kuroyukihime returned to Haruyuki and the others and gave instructions in a cool voice. "Everyone's health gauges, except for Magenta's, are basically less than half. We'll pull together here and fire on the enemy army assault, and then wipe them out in one go with all our Incarnate techniques."

"...Okay!" Haruyuki shuddered slightly.

Kuroyukihime and Pard hadn't been struggling with their attack on the enemy's left flank. Even as they were distracted by the Incarnate Dark Shots that kept coming from all directions, they still managed not to concentrate the damage they did on any one individual, instead uniformly bringing down the enemy army's health. Niko and Utai had done the same. And the four had avoided all Incarnate techniques while they did this, in order to reduce even a little the risk of calling Enemies to the scene.

What made something like this possible was the actual power of four high rankers, including two kings, but it was also because of the monotony of the enemy attack. Although the power contained in each blow was formidable, as long as you knew you were only facing the same attack over and over, handling it was simple. Even Haruyuki, who may or may not have finally been stepping out of newbie territory, had been able to repel single Dark Shots with near certainty.

Magenta. The fights in the new world you want likely would be fair. But they probably wouldn't be duels anymore. He clenched his hands at this fleeting thought and got into position.

The enemy knew at this point that Fuko and Akira would completely repel a simultaneous launch of Dark Shot, so there were likely no more long-distance attacks coming. They would finally come to settle the victory with an artless, all-out assault.

The clouds rolling along the horizon covered the massive evening sun of the Twilight stage, and the world was slightly obscured. A few seconds later, a red sunbeam poured down onto the battlefield through a break in the clouds.

Taking this as a signal, both sides moved. Still in their double-line formation, the Magenta army charged, making the ground shake. The Lotus army pulled into a *V* formation with Kuroyukihime at the tip, ready to welcome them with fire. Fourteen fists were wrapped in dark aura, and eight arms shot forward with overlays of various colors, only missing the yellow-green of Lime Bell. The total, localized activation of the Incarnate System sent bolts of pale lightning racing through the air.

However.

Just as the two armies were on the verge of their final clash, they were forcibly interrupted.

Rrrrr! Without warning, the ground began to ripple. Together with a roar that threatened to tear heaven and earth asunder, the intense vertical shaking thrust Haruyuki upward, and he reflexively spread his wings and reached out to support Kuroyukihime on his right and Takumu on his left. The Magenta army being in the middle of a charge was an additional catastrophe; they all tumbled into one massive tangle of arms and legs. The perfect chance to attack—but without the mental leeway to have the thought, Haruyuki looked around, dumbfounded.

There were no earthquakes or terrain effects in the Twilight stage. Which meant the tremor was due to something other than a stage attribute. But it couldn't have been a duel avatar ability, either. Shaking the indestructible earth of the stage on this massive a scale was simply impossible, no matter how large the avatar.

In which case, it could only have been the work of an Enemy, but in each direction, there was nothing but grass and a string of chalky temples.

"......Ah......Ah......!" A hoarse cry escaped Haruyuki's throat the instant he noticed *it*:

There *was* something.

In front of Midtown Tower, soaring up on the south side of the battlefield. There was something on top of the gentle hill. Almost entirely transparent but as big as a mountain: *something*. Unaware even that the shaking had stopped, Haruyuki simply stared at the thing.

Cracks radiated outward from the hill, with the destruction reaching even the tower wall to the rear. Most likely, the sudden, massive earthquake of a few seconds ago had its epicenter in that place. But had it really been an earthquake? The source of the tremor hadn't come from below the ground, but rather above—from the sky? In other words, perhaps the sudden shaking had been the shock wave from some massive thing—for instance, a super-large Enemy flying down from a distant height—hitting the top of Midtown Tower?

The moment his brain had made it this far, the something on

the hill shifted slowly. The outline drawn by the distortion of the red sunlight spread out to either side...almost like wings.

He had seen this curious silhouette before—humanlike, birdlike. It was without a doubt the shape he had seen from the roof of Roppongi Hills Tower ten days earlier.

This was the Legend-class Enemy, Archangel Metatron.

"...Kuroyukihime." Haruyuki squeezed a thin voice out of his blocked throat. "Metatron's on the ground."

"Wh—?"

Kuroyukihime's arm shook in Haruyuki's hand. Fuko, Akira, Niko, and everyone else all stared soundlessly at the hill to the south. After a moment, Magenta apparently noticed something going on with the Lotus army and looked back, hands still pressed against the ground. She, too, froze on the spot.

In the silence, the massive, invisible body casually took off from the top of the hill. *Go back to the Tower,* Haruyuki prayed in one corner of his numb mind. But the fantastic archangel slowly, ever so slowly, started toward them, as if sneering at this desperate prayer. Because it was so impossibly large, he couldn't get a sense of how far away it was. The transparent wings covered the entire sky.

"Everyone, retreat!!" Kuroyukihime shouted hoarsely, breaking free of the spell.

Haruyuki let go of his friends, whirled around, and began to run with his comrades. Three steps, four, five, and the ground shook once more. Metatron had landed. The shock wave was milder than the first one, but it was still forceful enough to sweep all of their feet out from under them. From the ground, Haruyuki looked over his shoulder and saw the grass flattened over a broad range not more than a hundred meters away. In precisely the midpoint between here and there, Magenta and the others also stood stock-still, dumbfounded.

Metatron's transparent wings emitted a hazy light.

The laser.

They wouldn't make it.

If they took a direct hit here...

The completed thought sparked in Haruyuki's brain and stirred his avatar. And not backward, but forward: "Run, everyone!!" he shouted and flew.

Skimming forward just barely above the ground, he crossed his arms in front of his body. *Kashk!* The armor of his forearm opened, and a transparent, light-guiding rod protruded from inside. When he touched down again, he didn't have time to think about why he chose a spot right next to Magenta Scissor and her gang.

A circle of light shone in the center of Metatron's round head. And then an intense glow, like a manifestation of divine will, jetted out silently. Haruyuki's field of view was dyed a uniform white. The evening of the stage, a screaming voice he could faintly hear—it all melted into the light and disappeared.

He couldn't see anything.

He couldn't feel anything.

His avatar had no doubt been completely evaporated. There was no way he could have succeeded. Reflecting Metatron's laser with this stopgap ability, when even the Green King could only defend against it for five seconds...

To begin with, Haruyuki hadn't managed to learn Theoretical Mirror, an absolute resistance to all light techniques, but Optical Conduction instead, the effects of which weren't nearly so definite. And yet, he had been so convinced that the technique he'd learned would work on Metatron, he had dragged his Legion members into this reckless mission. He had promised to protect them all, but he couldn't even withstand the terrible light for a single second. Not only would his avatar be burned up in it, but even his soul, and his very existence would be extinguished. Perhaps he would never be able to go anywhere again...

—*No.*

In a corner of the snowy-white world, he could see something.

Green like an emerald, long and thin like a sword, it was—a health gauge.

In the Unlimited Neutral Field, you couldn't see other people's gauges. Which meant that this was Haruyuki's—Silver Crow's—gauge. About 30 percent of it had been shaved away, but it definitely existed in the top left of his field of view.

He was still alive.

The instant he became aware of this, all sensation came flooding back to him. Light. Heat. Roaring. Pressure. The light-guiding rod of his crossed arms was shining intensely, shredding the unprecedented stream of energy in all directions. What had whisked away part of Haruyuki's gauge was not the laser itself, but the molten earth. The deflected laser had transformed the grassy field into a sea of flames, heating Crow's legs red-hot up to just below his knees.

The instant he caught a glance of this, he became aware— belatedly—of a ferocious pain magnified to twice that of the normal duel field, but he gritted his teeth and endured it. If he shifted or lost even the tiniest bit of ground, he would be beaten back by the relentless pressure and be evaporated this time, for sure.

"Hng...Ngh!!" A moan slipping out of his throat, Haruyuki desperately braced his legs. He didn't know how many seconds the laser attack would go on, but he would defend against it, right up to the end. Absolutely. He would not think negative thoughts again. He would not give up or say it was impossible. He would protect them: The comrades who had believed in him and come to this battlefield with him. Rin Kusakabe, fighting her own battle in the real world. And Ash Roller, the first friend he'd made in the Accelerated World.

But almost as if to sneer at this resolve, his feet slipped slightly. It wasn't just the grass; even the ground was starting to melt in the intense heat. If he used his wings, he could escape the conflagration, but the instant his feet left the ground, he would most likely lose his balance and be swallowed up by the laser. His only choice was to batten down the hatches where he was. Would Metatron's attack end first or would his feet lose their grip and take him down?

Zzsh. He slid backward again. The laser attack had already been going for more than five seconds, but it showed no signs of stopping. The longer he stood against it, the more the earth melted and sapped his health gauge and his footing. The soles of his feet had essentially lost all sensation of contact with the ground. He tried desperately to hold his position, but in the thin magma spreading out over the surface of the earth, his body leaned back bit by bit. He mustered every inch of power and balance he could to resist the pressure of the light. He couldn't fall now.

"Unh…Aaah…!" Crying out once more, Haruyuki mustered a little bit more strength at his edges to endure another second. But no matter how determined he might have been, the surface of the earth did not get the message; its melting did not stop. Burning bright red, his feet were essentially floating in the viscous liquid. His avatar inclined even farther. The laser reflected by his arms grew in strength, as if triumphant.

Is this it?

No, one more second.

At least until. Everyone. Escapes to…a safe…distance…!! Rather than giving up, Haruyuki shored up his resolve.

And then someone's hands were supporting his shoulders from behind.

Taku? Chiyu? Or maybe Kuroyukihime?

Dashing this fleeting thought was a voice in his ear.

"I'm here holding you up. You just focus on reflecting!"

That slightly husky voice. Magenta Scissor, who he'd only just been fiercely battling.

In what was basically an unconscious choice, Haruyuki had landed in a position that covered Magenta and her army when he took on the laser. Nearly ten seconds had passed since then. Magenta and her crew could have run a fair distance in that time, so why was she right behind him? And why was she helping him?

But he didn't have the brainpower to spare at the moment for such questions. There was an echo of great pain in Magenta's voice. Her feet were also being swallowed up by the magma. She probably wouldn't be able to support him for all that long.

"...Thanks!" he called briefly in reply, and leaned into her. His body stabilized, he now focused all his mental energy on his crossed arms.

Silver Crow's Optical Conduction ability used a light-guiding rod in his arm to change the vector of light-type attacks. It didn't compare with Mirror Masker's defensive power of turning his entire body into a mirror and reflecting light from all directions, but it did have one advantage over Theoretical Mirror—and it was that he could control, to a certain extent, the direction the laser was reflected.

Currently, the extremely thick laser was being scattered in a lenticular, which was why more than 30 percent of the energy was hitting the ground and producing the magma. But he should have been able to narrow the reflection vector and let the light flow off into the sky. If he did that, then the ground wouldn't melt any more than it already had.

The idea wasn't to become a wall that simply rejected the light. It was to be a path that accepted the light, guided it, and then released it. That was the answer Haruyuki had arrived at. Niko had taught him this, and Utai, and Kuroyukihime, and Wolfram Cerberus, and his classmate Reina Izeki; this was his ability and his alone: Optical Conduction.

You have to believe. In everyone. In me. In Silver Crow.

Haruyuki loosened his tightly clenched fists. Instantly, the pressure of the light beam increased, and his body slid back several centimeters together with Magenta. But he had faith in the strength of the hands supporting him and continued to lean into them. Now that he thought about it, the reason for the pain in Magenta's voice wasn't just the flames roasting her feet. She was also actively resisting the orders of the ISS kit parasitizing her chest.

He stretched out the fingers of his unclenched hands. The illumination filling the light-guiding rod reached down from the palm of his hand up to the tips of his middle fingers. Next, bit by bit, he moved his arms, already crossed into an X, into a vertical equal sign.

The beam of light became hundreds of small streams blowing off in all directions and then started to come back together piecemeal. Ten thick lines bundled together into four, joined into two, returned to one—toward the sky.

Now Haruyuki's arms shifted Metatron's giant light lance ninety degrees, sending the beam upward to be absorbed into the distant sky. Enormous holes were ripped into the clouds along its trajectory, making the evening darkness sparkle.

Right. Like that.

Abruptly, he heard someone's voice inside his mind. It seemed like a woman, but it wasn't Magenta. It had a childish aspect to it, but it wasn't Niko or Utai, either. Cool, inorganic, a voice slightly removed from humanity.

Just like that, reverse the light.

—Don't be absurd!! Haruyuki replied reflexively in his mind. *It's seriously way too hard just to bend Metatron's super-laser ninety degrees!! Now I'm just going to keep doing it and wait for his energy to run out!!*

It won't run out for a while. It collects sunlight with its wings. And the name isn't super-laser. Call it Trisagion.

* * *

—How do you know that? And to begin with...how are you talking...?

You don't have time to concern yourself with trivialities. Hurry, you must reverse the light. There is no other way for you all to survive.

—As if it's that easy! I mean, I'm slamming up against my limit here! Haruyuki threw these thoughts at the mysterious voice, but if its owner was right, then as long as Metatron was bathed in the light of the sun, its energy would continue to be charged. He had diverted the laser that was heating the ground up into the sky, but the magma at their feet still hadn't cooled, and his and Magenta's health gauges continued to decrease steadily.

—So that's my only choice, then...!

He had no basis for believing the unidentified voice, but he followed his instincts, and once again concentrated all his mental energy in his arms.

His arms were facing palm out and were bent deeply, in a shape like boxing gloves; he tried stretching them out just a little. The angle of the pillar of light reaching up into the sky changed the tiniest bit, but at the same time, an incredible pressure made his entire body creak. *It's totally impossible to make the angle of reflection any bigger than this,* he thought, before he remembered that only moments earlier, he'd sworn he absolutely would not give up, at least not in this fight. Hadn't he?

"Hn...nngh...!" A thin groan escaping him, Haruyuki extended his arms a little more. The laser's angle of reflection passed a hundred degrees, and his avatar began to shake irregularly. Supporting Crow from behind, Magenta had to be enduring even more serious pressure, but the hands gripping his shoulders didn't so much as twitch.

Once more, and again, Haruyuki bent the enormous pillar of light, what the mysterious voice had called Trisagion. The pressure also increased proportionally, unlimited, and sparks began to shoot like blood from Crow's joints. Magenta panted as if she were struggling, too, and both were pushed backward.

But at that moment, he heard yet another voice:

"Unh…unh…Aaaaah!" A thick war cry that didn't quite form words.

Zzsh! He felt the ground shake heavily, and then their backward slide stopped. Haruyuki couldn't see him, but Avocado Avoider had come up to brace Magenta with his massive body. But Avocado, clad in fatty armor, was weak to fire. The ground around them was still burning red-hot, and if he stood there, he would go up in flames in seconds.

"Unnh…Unh!" He was in anguish.

"Get back, Avo!" Magenta instructed hoarsely. "We're okay here. You run with everyone…"

"N-no, can't…! I'm…I'm a. B…Bur…"

His voice cut off there, but Haruyuki knew what Avocado Avoider was trying to say. *I'm a Burst Linker, too.* That's what he wanted to declare.

"Avo…," Magenta murmured.

The crackling roar of the flames drowned her out. Avocado's armor had probably started to burn. Haruyuki had maybe ten seconds left. Could he bend the laser 180 degrees before that…?

Fwwsh! White smoke rose up from the earth. Stunned, Haruyuki looked down at his feet and found that most of the red-hot magma had hardened to black in an instant. Someone had thrown a large amount of water on it. But the Twilight stage was essentially dry; the only water was in places that corresponded to large ponds or rivers in the real world. Where on earth had this much liquid come from?

He turned his head slightly, and entering Haruyuki's field of view was Aqua Current, missing the majority of the flowing water armor that was her lifeline. Laid bare, the avatar's body was a transparent material like crystal. She had used the water that covered her to cool the ground.

"We're late." Akira reached out her extremely thin arms to support Haruyuki's back from the left of Magenta Scissor.

"Sorry, Crow." New arms wrapped around his back from the right. "Magenta's comrades couldn't move. It took us a while to carry them to a safe place."

Kuroyukihime. And then on either side of these two—Takumu, Chiyuri, Fuko, Utai, Niko, Pard all stretched out their arms to form a tight scrum with Magenta and Avocado.

"We're counting on you, Crow!" Takumu cried.

"Up to you now! Crush it!!" Niko shouted.

With two Enemies and eight allies—no, ten Burst Linkers—supporting him, Haruyuki nodded to the extent possible and then turned his resolve back to Metatron's laser.

The members of the Magenta army, other than Avocado, had likely fallen because of the clash between the orders the ISS kits were giving and their own wills. In other words, in their hearts, they too wanted to come fight together, like Magenta and Avocado. To protect their comrades from the sudden threat assaulting them. No matter how the ISS kits polluted their minds, it could not extinguish the flames at the very depths of their souls. As long as they were Burst Linkers, those would never disappear.

"Unh...Ah..." Squeezing a groan from his throat, Haruyuki pushed his arms forward bit by tiny bit. The force pressing in on him threatened to instantly crush his avatar if his focus so much as wavered, but there was no longer any doubt in his heart.

When the angle of reflection had reached 120 degrees, the bent laser touched the tip of Midtown Tower. The marble wall was instantly red-hot, melting and shattering. Almost like a divine sword being brought down from on high, the laser cut the massive chalky tower in two. A terrain object of that size was, as a general rule, indestructible in the Unlimited Neutral Field, and yet, this laser had slid through it so easily; it was indeed a fearsome power.

The laser destroyed only one part of the building, fifty meters wide, but there was also the chance that the ISS kit main body somewhere on the upper floors had been hit directly. If he moved the laser from side to side, that probability would increase, but that, at least, was firmly outside the realm of possibility. He was mustering every ounce of his physical and mental energy, and yet it was all he could do to bring his arms straight down.

Yes. Don't think of anything else.

He heard the voice again. That inorganic...and somehow inhuman voice didn't even quaver despite coming in the midst of destruction so great that it was enough to split a landmark of the Accelerated World.

Keep going down. Aim for the laser's emission point. Anything else will pass through.

—*Pass through...?* At this, Haruyuki finally remembered: Archangel Metatron was invisible outside of a Hell stage...and *all attacks passed through it.* But the mysterious voice was telling him there *was* a place where Metatron could take damage, even in this Twilight stage. This information didn't come out at the meeting of the Seven Kings; which meant that the owner of the voice knew things that even the Seven Kings—no, the first Burst Linkers known as the Originators—didn't.

Who in the world was it? The thought bubbled up in a corner of his mind, bounced, and disappeared. He only had the will left now to simply and precisely follow its instructions.

A hundred fifty degrees. A hundred sixty...A hundred seventy.

Already some percentage of the laser was overlapping with itself on the return trip, and he couldn't keep his eyelids up in the dazzling light that the colliding energy released. The world was dyed in light and shadow, and Silver Crow's arms bringing about this phenomenon shone with a pure-white light. It seemed like they would explode with the light-guiding rod at any second, but there was no fear inside Haruyuki. His hips, his back, both were being supported by eight—no, just for right now, ten friends. He felt their wills filling his avatar and giving him strength.

One hundred seventy-five degrees.

The bottom edge of the reflected laser touched the transparent head of Metatron. The outline only shone a little more brightly; nothing else happened. Not moving in the slightest, the large Enemy continued to fire its laser. But Haruyuki believed in himself and his friends and the mysterious voice, and continued to push his arms down. His elbows were already essentially straight. Carefully turning his arms, his palms up…With fingers snapped straight, he shot through the laser's origin point.

One hundred eighty degrees.

Something happened.

At first, that was all he could feel. There was no explosion or roar, but he felt the laser—which should have continued to pass right through the Enemy—hit a small something. The pillar of light gradually decayed. The pressure weighing heavily on his entire body slowly slackened. It weakened, and then got still weaker…and disappeared.

Before he knew it, the pure-white radiance that had encompassed his field of view, the vibrating noise that drowned out all other sound, had vanished like they never existed. All he could hear was the sound of rubble falling in the distance from the cross section of Midtown Tower, that reached from the roof almost down to the base.

No, that wasn't all: There was a strange noise, too, like the creaking of a large chunk of ice suddenly melting. *Krak-krak, skree-skree.* The foreboding sound steadily grew louder. And it seemed like Haruyuki wasn't the only one who heard it; the clump of ten at his back also strained their ears, motionless.

Inside Haruyuki's mind as he stood stock-still, he could hear that voice yet again.

*   *   *

It all starts now.
You must all fight with your entire might.

Skreeee!

The sound of collision threatened to rip the field itself apart—like the sound of acceleration when you called the Burst Link command, but amplified a thousand times.

And then Haruyuki saw it. Fifty meters away, the shell of space split and a figure appeared from inside.

What appeared first were widespread wings. Not those of a bird of prey. And they were different from Crow's metallic fins, too. Looking like numerous complex tapestries all lined up, these wings had a span as great as the breadth of Midtown Tower. And there were two each on the right and left, for a total of four. The torso beneath the wings was composed of countless connected white rings. Beneath the torso, more than ten tube-shaped legs stretched out.

And the head was a massive sphere, perhaps seven, eight meters in diameter. This alone was basically the size of a Beast-class Enemy. Along the surface of the sphere, curving lines radiated outward and came together in one spot in the front, but this area alone was black, caved in. Probably where the organ to launch the laser—no, Trisagion—had been.

On the top of the round head sat a crown-like ring that shone platinum silver. And from the center of that, a curiously shaped horn stretched up. At a distance, he couldn't see the details of the chaotic silhouette.

Haruyuki had confirmed this much when Kuroyukihime moved smoothly away from supporting his back. "There's no mistake," she announced, her voice quiet but still maximally tense. "That is the Legend-class Enemy, Archangel Metatron."

Hearing this, the other nine slowly pulled away from Haruyuki. Finally, Haruyuki lowered the arms still crossed in front of him.

"Magenta Scissor," Kuroyukihime murmured. "Can we hold off on our contest for a while? We must defeat this Enemy."

"Why don't you run?" Magenta replied in a similarly quiet voice. "I think you could escape now, yes?"

"If we run now, Crow's hard work is for nothing. We've sealed away the laser, which is this monster's greatest weapon. And its transparency has also been released. There is no time but now. After we defeat Metatron, we can recommence our fight if you wish."

"…" After a slight silence, Magenta said to him, "The arrogance, hmm, just like the rumors. But…just this once, I'm not annoyed. We'll fight another day…Let's go, Avo."

Magenta turned on her heel, and Avocado slowly roused himself to go after her, both of them still with the ISS kits on their chests, although the lids were half-closed. Which meant that the kit main body had not taken a direct hit and was still going strong somewhere inside that building.

In that moment, he honestly didn't understand how they had fought the control of the kit, but he could say this at the very least: Magenta Scissor and Avocado Avoider had not abandoned their pride as Burst Linkers. Just that.

"Um, thank you, Magenta!" Haruyuki managed to call out toward her back as she started to walk to the north. "If you hadn't held me up, I would have been evaporated."

"…We both would have. And I'll say a thank you for helping my friends."

As she and Avocado walked away, Haruyuki saw their lower halves were scorched by the heat of the magma.

Magenta had to have understood. That the reason Haruyuki and his friends were fighting Metatron was to destroy the ISS kit main body inside Midtown Tower. And that once the main body was destroyed, the kit terminals that gave her and her comrades their strength would all lose that power.

Haruyuki saw the two of them off, an indescribable feeling in his heart. But he wasn't given the time to sit with it.

Vsshn. An earth-shattering noise shook the field, and he whirled around.

Perhaps recovered from being shot in the head with its own laser, Metatron started to lumber forward. Haruyuki couldn't see anything that looked like eyes anywhere, but even so, he felt a powerful gaze. An inorganic will to eliminate anyone who invaded its own territory.

"This is the critical moment of today's mission." Kuroyukihime stated, her voice clear with no hint of the exhaustion she must have felt. "Although we've sealed away the laser that is its main weapon, that does not change the fact that Metatron is a fearsome Enemy. But we must defeat it. Absolutely. Now, after Crow took on such an important role with such resolve and determination, we must match his efforts—"

"So basically, don't go giving Burst Linkers a bad name!!" Waiting for the perfect moment to shout this out was, of course, Niko. Clenching her right hand into a fist, she thrust it at Metatron, who was steadily shambling forward. "I am so seriously on fire right now. Those ISS kit kids, they showed some serious guts. You guys, if we don't put the fight up now, we might as well close up shop as Legions! Got it? No holding back! Knock that giant lump outta the park!"

To Niko's king-upstaging speech, Utai immediately added:

"We're gonna smack 'im good!"

The two red types had apparently gotten fairly close that day. In response, the other seven—with Kuroyukihime sounding just a little bit grumpy—all agreed, "Yeah!"

7

In the battle strategy they had agreed on at the old Tokyo Tower, they were to avoid direct combat with Archangel Metatron to the best of their abilities. While Haruyuki was defending against the laser, the others would charge into Midtown Tower.

But now that Metatron had descended, they were forced to essentially scrap that plan. It seemed doubtful that the Enemy would stop targeting them once they ran into the tower, and in the worst-case scenario, they might get caught between an enemy lying in wait inside and Metatron prowling around outside.

In unexpected good news, however, Metatron could not fire the large-diameter laser—supposedly its most powerful attack—and its usual status of being immune to all damage had been stripped away. As long as these two factors were taken out of play, it was actually possible to fight Metatron in something other than a Hell stage. Naturally, they couldn't underestimate the power of a Legend-class Enemy, but at the very least, Metatron was no longer on the unfathomable level of the Super-class Enemies of the Castle.

More than anything, if they could defeat the Enemy here, when it next regenerated, it would be back in its original territory, the deepest level of the Shiba Park Dungeon. It still wasn't clear who had moved Metatron from there to the top of Midtown Tower, but it wouldn't be easy to manage that feat twice. In other words, even if they didn't manage to complete their mission to destroy the ISS kit main body that day, they could at least leave the tower defenseless for a while.

For these reasons, the nine Burst Linkers took on the challenge of a decisive battle with the Archangel.

Two minutes and thirty seconds after the assault began, Haruyuki—and probably his friends, too—were made powerfully aware of how soft their initial estimations had been.

"Wing attack's coming! Get ready to evade!"

At Kuroyukihime's instruction, the vanguard of Haruyuki, Takumu, Fuko, and Pard quickly jumped back and looked up at the sky. Above them, Metatron's main four wings were spread wide. The feathers, twelve tapestries on each wing, shimmered with blue light. *Ksha!* The air split and all twelve shot down to the ground like lightning bolts.

The feathers were more than a meter wide, but thin like paper, and easily sliced through the armor of any avatar they touched. They whizzed through the air, their trajectories completely random, and Haruyuki and the others did everything they could to slip around and past them. Thin blue blades shot down one after another and dug deeply into the surface of the earth.

"Crow, watch out!" A voice cried out from behind him just when he thought he'd dodged them all.

An intense impact—but he took basically no damage. He looked back and saw Takumu holding up his right arm as he pushed Haruyuki aside. The tip of a sharp feather had pierced his Enhanced Armament and made it all the way through the thick plating to the avatar's body. The pile driver, the symbol of Cyan Pile, was already battered and beaten after the spike had been transformed into a two-handed sword for the Incarnate technique Cyan Blade—not to mention blocking any number of Metatron's attacks. Yet, it was still in one piece for now; the pummeled pile had not lost its shine.

When the forty-eight feathers were pulled back up into the air, Haruyuki slapped his hand on Takumu's back and shouted, "Sorry, Pile!"

"It's okay. I can still keep going!" His close friend's words were reassuring, but there was a hint of exhaustion in his voice.

Haruyuki himself was aware of his focus getting worse. That he had missed the feather attacking from behind was proof of that. His health gauge still had more than 60 percent left, after the damage he took defending against the laser, but if his movement got any duller, it would be cut down to the red zone in an instant.

"Pile, hold on just a sec!" Chiyuri shouted from where she was stationed to the rear in the middle guard. "As soon as my gauge charges, I'll heal you!"

"Got it!" Takumu waved his hand in response.

In a long Enemy battle, there was nothing more reliable than Citron Call. But the technique seriously ate up Chiyuri's special-attack gauge, and there were basically no objects in the area that could be destroyed. Thus, even she needed to get close during the slim openings with Metatron and charge her gauge through direct attacks. Since they couldn't lose Lime Bell, Akira was guarding her, but she was still without the majority of her flowing water armor, so they had to plan their assault timing carefully.

After the completion of the cutting-feather attack—this also likely had an official name like Trisagion, but the mysterious voice hadn't said a word since the start of the battle—Metatron's four wings folded back. That was when the beast was assailed by countless flames, drawing out parabolas in the sky.

This was Niko and Utai from the rear, the group's long-range attack squad. The rocket missiles of the Red King, who had once again summoned the armored trailer Dreadnought, and the fissioning flame arrows of Maiden's special attack, Flame Torrents, blanketed the Archangel's massive body. Dozens of small explosions made the stage shake, and the first level of the Enemy's four-level health gauge disappeared without a sound.

Still three levels to go...

Haruyuki shook off the thought that flickered through his mind and leapt off the ground. He joined up with Kuroyukihime and Chiyuri and the others who came racing over and launched his Aerial Combo, hovering next to Metatron's torso. The matte, snowy-white structure felt to his hands like he was punching sturdy ceramic composite, and it neither cracked nor dented. But he believed that each blow brought the gauge down however little, and he put his all into every punch, kick, and spin.

"Crow, you're going too far!"

He heard Kuroyukihime call out abruptly, and he opened his eyes wide. Without his realizing it, innumerable tiny holes had opened up all over the seven-meter head sitting on top of the long torso.

"Ngh...!" Guarding his body with his arms, he folded the wings on his back. His avatar was pulled downward by the virtual gravity, but not fast enough.

Tight, snail-like spirals poked their faces out from the openings in Metatron's round head. *Ta-ta-ta-ta-ta-tat!* The spiral bullets shot out, machine-gun fire in all directions.

They had learned that the instant the holes appeared, they needed to immediately stop their attack and take cover in the one place the bullets didn't reach—underneath Metatron's torso. But Haruyuki had been late to retreat, and he was hit in the right arm and left hip, which knocked him to the ground. The white snails kept rotating for a while even after impact, and they dug deep into Crow's silver armor, sending orange sparks and red damage effects shooting outward.

"Nngah—!" The pain was dizzyingly intense.

Clawed hands yanked him up.

Blood Leopard. From the fang-filled mouth, a stern order was issued in a tone that brooked no argument: "Crow, long-range with Rain and the others."

"Huh...? I-I'm okay. I can still—"

"Get back, Corvus." A new voice interrupted his rebuttal. "We'll call you up again soon."

When even Fuko was telling him to fall back, there was no point in arguing it. He could throw a tantrum, but it would only expose everyone else to danger.

"…I'm sorry!" Haruyuki shouted just this, and somehow managed to return the nod from Kuroyukihime, who was watching him with concerned eyes, before spreading his wings. He flew back to where Niko and Utai had set up camp, about fifty meters to the rear.

The instant he landed beside the tank, all the strength drained out of his legs and he dropped to his knees. His exhaustion was apparently greater than he'd thought.

Dammit! At such an important time! He tried desperately to stand, but—

"C, please rest a little." Utai wrapped a small hand around his shoulder. "That is also important work."

"That's right, Crow!" Niko's voice came over the speaker. *"You've already done some seriously fine work. You leave the rest to us!"*

Their kindness made him happy but also frustrated at the same time, and Haruyuki clenched his hands as tightly as he could.

He'd been faintly aware that he was not good with long battles. Even in his daily normal duels, if the fight time exceeded twenty minutes, his chances of victory dropped significantly. He was good at hyper-accelerating his senses in the critical moment, but the flip side of that was he couldn't really show off his full power in situations that required a fixed concentration for a long period.

It was the same in the real world. He managed somehow to get through the homework every day, but even when he decided to voluntarily study for a long period, he would end up staring into space after two or three hours, and the meaning of the numbers and letters no longer registered in his mind.

He knew he couldn't keep going like that. With his current

scholastic abilities, there probably wasn't any point in even talking about achieving the biggest objective he'd ever had in his life, the goal he secretly harbored in his heart—going to the same high school as Kuroyukihime in two years. For that, he would need to study diligently on his own and bring up his grades now, while he was still in eighth grade, but no matter what he did, his brain's energy just wouldn't last.

"You mustn't rush," Utai noted quietly, almost as if reading his mind. "One little thing, another, another, and then another. If you build your work up like this, you'll reach your goal someday. No matter how far away or great it might be, I'm certain of it. C, you must already be aware of this."

As Haruyuki lifted his face, the small shrine maiden drew her longbow. A smooth, effortless motion; calm, relaxed. The ultimate in refinement, backed by thousands, tens of thousands of repetitions.

She launched the flame arrow with a call of the technique name. It turned into a red shooting star and flew through the evening sky, splitting soundlessly. The flaming meteor shower rained down on the massive Enemy with terrifying precision.

One small thing, one at a time.

"...Right. If you're tired, I guess you should rest," Haruyuki muttered. He relaxed his clenched fists and let all the tension slip out of his body. Strangely, the sensation came back into his weak legs. "It was like that when I was cleaning Hoo's hut, too. I didn't try to clean everything right from the start. I thought of things I *could* do and got a little further, and then a little further, and then before I knew it, it was all finished."

Utai said nothing, but a faint smile rose up on her face. Or so he felt.

Haruyuki stood up slowly and took a deep breath. The exhaustion was still there. But that was only natural. To repel Metatron's laser, he had pushed his powers of concentration to the absolute limit. Right now, he had to do the things he could here.

He reached out the fingers of his right hand and generated a silver overlay in them. He built it slowly, without hurrying. Once it was large enough, he stretched his arm out in front of him. Slowly, slowly, he pulled it back.

Now, where to aim?

Laser Javelin, the sole long-distance attack available to Haruyuki, did not have a high accuracy. But Metatron was enormous. He should be able to aim for the wings, torso, or head.

Coolly, he observed the Enemy's body. If it had a weak point, it would have been the strangely shaped horn stretching out from the top of its round head, but that was definitely too small a target. The next thing that stood out was the crown on the top of its head. When looked at closely, the crown alone, out of all the parts of Metatron's body, was not white, but rather silver.

Try to hit it?

Eyes fixed on the platinum circlet and careful not to exert himself, Haruyuki pulled his right arm back to just before his shoulder. The silver lance produced itself in midair, trembling slightly. If Haruyuki wanted force, he would call out the name of the technique here and increase his image of it with that trigger. But right now, what he wanted more than power was accuracy; if he yelled, that would knock his aim off. Mouth closed, he gently cut the base of the lance free with his left hand.

The Incarnate lance flew, trailing silver light. Anytime he'd used it before, it had carved out a spiral trajectory, but just this once, it was flying in what was basically a straight line. Metatron had stopped for the wing attack, and the lance was sucked soundlessly into the crown tightly encircling its head.

Skeeenk! The clear metallic squeal reached even Haruyuki's distant ears. At the same time, it looked as though the Enemy's massive body stiffened, if only for a moment.

And then he heard the voice again.

Yes. That is good. Continue to aim for the same location.

—What? You're still here? Why didn't you say anything?

*   *   *

You were not listening. From now on, turn your ears this way and do exactly as I say.

Who died and made you king? he couldn't help thinking. The formal nature of the speech was totally different from Utai's. Once again, he felt the question of who exactly this voice belonged to, but it didn't seem like this was the best time to take his eyes off Metatron. At the very least, if the voice was giving him advice, it wasn't an enemy.

"Rain, Mei!" Haruyuki turned to Utai and Niko. "That crown thing on Metatron's forehead seems to be a weak point. Let's all concentrate our fire there."

"Where's the forehead?! And where do you get off bossing me around?!" Even as she yelled at him, Niko turned her main armaments a little to the left. Utai also lowered the sights on her longbow.

"We'll all fire together. I'll count down." Bringing the light into his right hand once more, Haruyuki continued, "Four, three, two, one, zero!"

Bright ruby-red lines gushed forward from the two laser guns, a large flame arrow shot forth from the longbow, and a lance of light was released from Haruyuki's hand. The three long-range techniques gradually closed in bit by bit, flying across the fifty meters, before fusing right in front of Metatron and slamming into the silver crown.

A high-pitched metallic shriek rang out, dozens of times louder than the previous hit. Kuroyukihime and the others on the front line leapt back in surprise. The massive Enemy body twisted in anguish; the wings fluttered open and closed.

"Wh-whoa…It worked…"

"It worked!" Utai agreed.

Nodding, Haruyuki sank into thought. If a long-distance attack was this effective, then a direct attack from close range would do even more damage to the crown. He unconsciously

took a step forward, but then stopped. He'd been ordered to the rear by both Pard and Fuko; he couldn't exactly just go back to the front line on his own—

"*Get in there*," Niko said abruptly, her voice containing a wry smile.

"Huh? But..."

"*You're relaxed, you're good. Or is that it? You not gonna obey the order of a king?*"

"O-of course! ...I understand. I'll go." Resolving himself, Haruyuki spread the wings on his back. "...Thanks, Rain, Mei!"

He kicked hard off the ground, strength now returned to his legs, and used his nearly full special-attack gauge to plunge toward the chaos around Metatron without holding back. Even as he flew along at top speed, the mysterious quiet in his heart didn't go away. Normally, his field of view would always narrow down to the single point of his objective, but now not only was Metatron itself perfectly clear, but so were the developments around it with the vanguard team, the middle guard a little farther back, and even the half-destroyed Midtown Tower in the background.

Still raging, the Enemy spread its four wings—the feather cutter attack. The sharp, thin films shone blue, and Kuroyukihime and the others on the ground readied to dodge.

Looking at them from above, he saw that the wings were deployed in an *X* shape, but there was a slight opening in the middle, at the back. He should be able to slip through that gap and reach the head. Cutting back and forth from right turn to sharp left, Haruyuki carefully examined his assault course.

Ksha! The forty-eight feathers shot outward. While the four members of the vanguard on the ground determinedly evaded the feather blades that gouged into the earth, Haruyuki plunged forward from Metatron's backside. He slipped through the gap in the wings and closed in on the round head.

The seven-meter diameter of the sphere was unfathomably large up close. Spiraling lines raced across the surface, and holes were burned not just into the front but the very rear as well. On the top sat the platinum silver crown, with a two-meter-long horn jutting up over the edge.

Without hesitation, Haruyuki grabbed onto the crown and launched a straight punch with his right fist, which bore the full thrust of his wings. A loud reverberation rang out, like a massive bell being struck. The sound waves radiated outward, making the twilight air shudder. Metatron's enormous body twisted violently, and almost as though its nervous system had gone awry, it flailed its many legs and wings.

Grabbing onto the crown tightly with both hands so he wouldn't be thrown off, Haruyuki shouted to Kuroyukihime and the others on the ground, "I'm attacking the crown! You guys keep attacking the body when Metatron starts to rampage!" He thought they would get mad at him for coming back without being asked, but they didn't.

"K!" Pard responded instantly, and everyone else also voiced their agreement to the plan.

Haruyuki pushed back the impulse to start whaling recklessly on the crown; he needed to wait for the right timing. If he could prevent Metatron's attacks by hammering at its weak point, then he should aim for the moment when it started the feather cutter or the snail shooter. Still clinging to the crown, he focused on the Enemy's movements.

Seen from up close, the platinum crown had a strange design, several C-shaped parts all joined together, but the tapered ends turned inward rather than out. Thanks to this, they were like handles, making it easy for Haruyuki to hang on. But the sharp, tapered ends cut into Metatron's white armor plate, and he wondered if it didn't hurt.

But even as he considered this detail, 80 percent of his mind was carefully taking in every aspect of the Enemy; he wouldn't miss the start of an attack. The rings that made up the body, each nearly two meters in diameter, began to spin at high speed. Purple sparks crackled in the several centimeters between the rings, forming air gaps. It was an area of effect electrical-discharge attack. Unlike Seiryu's Thunder Blast, this one spread out horizontally, so unless you immediately went into a frantic full dash to get some real distance the moment you saw the first inklings of the attack, you couldn't escape it.

But the four members of the vanguard trusted Haruyuki and stayed in close range. He couldn't let them down. Taking his hands away from the crown, Haruyuki hovered and plunged his right fist—and unconsciously its overlay—into the joint between two C shapes.

The sound of impact nearly deafened him. Tiny cracks raced outward along the platinum surface, and Metatron howled soundlessly, its body writhing. The electricity, on the verge of being fired, discharged spontaneously and pierced the hollow body cavity, back and forth and then back to the other side again.

"Errrrng…yaaah!" The battle cry was Kuroyukihime's. Jumping high up into the air, she yelled, "Death By Piercing!!"

The special attack shot out from her right hand to shatter one of Metatron's legs. The other three—realizing perhaps that it was now or never—also launched an all-out assault with one attack after another. From the rear, lasers and fire arrows precision-sniped the torso, and they dug deeper down into the second level of the Enemy's health gauge.

Normally, this would be where he did a fist pump with a "Yeah!" but the strange sensation that filled his mind threatened to disappear, so Haruyuki instead readied himself for the next attack.

He was maintaining a wide field of view, but it was different from being scattered. It was like he could now control with his own will all the focus that, up to that point, he'd only been able to pour into a single moment, a single instant. Accelerating full throttle was only good for those "now or never" moments. Until then, he would be quietly ready, watch the whole situation, and move smoothly.

Having recovered from the damage, Metatron went into a

normal attack with its legs and tail. As they evaded these blows, Kuroyukihime and the others darted in to counterattack. Once this offense/defense had gone on for about ten seconds, the Enemy yanked its upper body upward. Countless holes opened up on the head, directly before Haruyuki's eyes.

If Silver Crow's whole body was showered by the spiral bullets at this close range, he wouldn't be able to avoid immediate death. But unhurried, Haruyuki aimed for the moment when Metatron stopped moving and shot a right-hand strike forward, enhanced with Incarnate.

He hit in the same place as the last time, and the cracks in the crown expanded. Spiral bullets sporadically launched from Enemy's head as it roared in anguish, but they had neither number nor force, so Haruyuki was able to defend easily enough with his arms.

The battle continued at a fixed pace, and Metatron's health gauge was gradually but definitely decreasing. The second tier, then the third, disappeared, and once they'd dug into the fourth tier, the attack pattern increased, but Haruyuki continued to fulfill his chosen role without panicking. The crown was also gradually destroyed, and then about forty-five minutes after the start of the fight…

The first thing to shatter was the platinum crown adorning Metatron's head. Haruyuki's hand strike completely pulverized one of the C-shaped rings, and instantly, the rest came apart and clattered separately to the ground.

From the pattern thus far, Haruyuki had anticipated that this would be the beginning of the final wild rampage, but unexpectedly, the Enemy stopped moving completely. Kuroyukihime also seemed confused for a moment, but the order for a full-scale attack came flying soon enough. Chiyuri and Akira also took part, and light effects of all colors enveloped the massive body.

Each time a large technique exploded, the fourth level of the gauge, now dyed red, was visibly carved away, until finally, sliced through from belly to back by Kuroyukihime's Incarnate technique Vorpal Strike, the Legend-class Enemy Archangel Metatron collapsed with a howl.

The white plates that made up its body slowly melted away, turning into particles of light from the ends. The spherical head broke apart, and light gushed out from inside.

Noting a message about the addition of a large number of points scrolling across the left side of his vision, Haruyuki jumped down to the ground.

"You did it, Crow!" Chiyuri came flying at him from behind and tousled his helmet.

Here, his supply of concentration finally exhausted, Haruyuki very nearly slumped to the ground.

"Whoopsy!" Chiyuri immediately reached to support him, lending him her shoulder to prop him up.

"Sh-shanks," he replied. When he lifted his head, he found the smiles—or rather just the sense of smiles, of course—on the helmets of Kuroyukihime, Takumu, Akira, Fuko, and Pard. They all started to say, "Good—" and then exchanged glances before ceding the right to speak to their commander.

Clearing her throat, Kuroyukihime took the floor. "Good work, Crow. That was some excellent fighting. You stepped up another level."

"N-no, that's…" He shrank into himself, and Chiyuri gave him a whack on the back.

"Stand tall at a time like this, at least!"

"G-got it. So don't pound on my back." He took a deep breath and stood up straight, still leaning on Chiyuri. He could see the pair in the rear guard through the gap between Kuroyukihime and Fuko. Utai, on top of Niko's tank, was waving wildly.

He went to raise his right hand in response, and then abruptly realized that there was something strange about the way Utai was waving. Less celebrating a victory, and more "watch out." When he looked very closely, the headlights on the trailer were also flashing on and off. Wondering what was going on, Haruyuki casually turned his face toward the sky.

Something curious floated soundlessly there. A white spindle that tapered to the top and bottom. A long, thin sash was wrapped diagonally around it, hiding the contents. The whole thing was about two meters long. The complicated patterns on the surface glittered beautifully in the evening sun.

I've seen that somewhere— Haruyuki's narrowed eyes flew wide open.

It was Metatron's horn. The protrusion that had an unknown use and stretched out from the round head still lingered in the sky, even after the annihilation of the Enemy.

"Wh-what is the meaning of this...?" Even Kuroyukihime sounded dumbfounded, following Haruyuki's gaze up toward the floating horn. "We defeated Metatron..."

"I checked the points addition. We definitely defeated it." Akira's voice was also slightly more tense than usual.

Then:

Inside his mind came the mysterious voice he'd heard any number of times during the fight.

What you all destroyed is nothing more than half my body.

Fwsh. The sash covering the horn opened up. Though—it wasn't a sash. It was long, supple wings. Four pairs.

Emerging from within was a girl, body wrapped in beautiful armor and garb. The whole of her was a pure-white, not a single blemish to be seen. Her hair, her skin, her clothes, they were all matte-white like snow; and half of her was colored orange like the evening sun, the other half the purple of dusk. Even though her eyes were closed, the beautiful girl was otherworldly. Giving off no sense of a life force at all, but not a simple object either, she had a bizarre presence.

Slowly, supply, both arms were spread out. Lids edged with white eyelashes cracked open the merest hint, and golden eyes took in the seven people on the ground.

An almost violent pressure slammed into him, and Haruyuki's

knees nearly gave way. He desperately braced himself, but he couldn't stop his trembling legs. Chiyuri shrieked slightly in her throat, and Kuroyukihime and the others were entirely stiff. This pressure-like aura was without a doubt approaching the territory of a Legend-class Enemy—no, even a Super-class Enemy. In other words—

This girl herself was the true form of Archangel Metatron.

In his mind, which threatened to shut down in the extreme shock and shivering fear, Haruyuki struggled to understand. Things were clearly not lining up. The voice that had given Haruyuki advice any number of times in the middle of the fight with the massive Metatron, its owner was Metatron's main body. What did that *mean*? Wasn't it basically that this female-shaped Enemy had told Haruyuki her own weak point and made him defeat her? His doubts only increased his fear. "H…how…?"

And then he heard the voice again.

Little bird. You succeeded in destroying the disgusting yoke that bound me. It is my destiny to burn up soldiers, but I shall turn a blind eye this time. Although, if you all wish to fight, then that is something else.

"W-w-we…don't wish to!" Haruyuki shouted in a trance.

The snowy-white archangel closed her eyelids once more and nodded placidly.

Well then, after a stroll through the lower world, I shall return to my Castle. Let us meet again someday, little ones.

The four wings wrapped one after another around her body, and Metatron returned to her spindle shape, her cocoon, before suddenly becoming a pillar of white flames and disappearing as though she had been completely burned up.

When the pressure that very nearly crushed him weakened and finally disappeared, Haruyuki staggered and crumpled to the ground. This time, Chiyuri did not offer support, but plopped

down with him. It seemed that the threat had passed, but he was still left not understanding anything. He cocked his head from side to side.

"...So then, is it something like this...?" Takumu broke the short silence, his eyes still on the sky. After this preamble, he continued, although he didn't sound too confident, "The reason Metatron was guarding Midtown Tower was because someone—probably a member of the Acceleration Research Society—tamed her, but she was against it. And then the crown on Metatron's head was what that girl called a yoke—in other words, some kind of tool or something for taming, and when Crow broke it, she could be free."

"Oh...Ohhh, I get it!" Haruyuki cried out, still sitting on ground. "Now that you mention it, just the crown wasn't white. It was silver."

This also explained why Metatron's main body had ordered Haruyuki to aim for the crown with telepathy or whatever. *If that was it, then you should've said so right from the start!* he unconsciously called toward the sky, but of course, there was no response.

Kuroyukihime also nodded as though Takumu's explanation made sense to her and looked at Fuko next to her. "At any rate, Raker, Curren, when we fought Metatron in the Contrary Cathedral, there was no main body like that, right?"

"There was not. Which means that what we thought we defeated was..."

"Only Metatron's lower half."

Chiyuri, still slumped on the ground next to Haruyuki, murmured, "So then, if we had defeated the massive part before Crow broke the tame crown...then, next we would've had to fight that girl?"

"Mm. It's possible..."

The members of the Black Legion sank into silence, while Pard looked over at Haruyuki and said, "GJ."

At this, he felt reassured that the battle was truly over and let out a deep breath. He hauled himself to his feet and lent Chiyuri a hand before turning his eyes toward Niko and Utai, who were on standby fifty meters away. The main guns of the trailer were turned in their direction, and Utai also had her longbow at the ready.

"Rain! Mei!" He waved and shouted loudly. "It's okay now! Please come over here!"

"You gotta say something sooner!" Niko's yell, amplified by the speaker, reached them with an assist from the wind, and he shrank into himself at the very reasonable nature of her request.

Utai leapt to the ground from the roof, and the weaponized trailer rumbled as it disassembled and melted into the air, disappearing. A small avatar dropped down from the cockpit area and stretched long and hard. The two red types clasped hands tightly before heading over to the others. Unsurprisingly, they looked exhausted; their footsteps were a little unstable, but linked by their hands, they continued to walk, supporting each other. Haruyuki felt something warm spread out in his heart at the sight.

When they were moving on the Castle for the mission to rescue Aqua Current, Utai had asked Haruyuki, *Do you remember, C?* The question was in reference to what Haruyuki had said to her when they were trapped inside the Castle. *I have a friend I'd like to introduce you to one day.* That friend was the very Niko walking alongside Utai at that moment.

There didn't seem to be any need for it now, but he would introduce them properly once the mission was entirely over. And Hoo in the rear courtyard, too. Niko would definitely like that. And then they could all go check out the student council's show together…

Haruyuki watched over the girls, these thoughts running through his mind, while ahead of him, Utai and Niko stepped into the long shadow of Midtown Tower stretching across the grassy field.

Sheenk.

Something flashed. On the roof of a low building far to the rear of the girls walking side by side. Not a reflection of the evening sun. A vivid-purple light, almost garish.

I've seen that light before. That was the only thought he had time for.

In the next instant, four beams of light soundlessly pierced the chest of Ardor Maiden. Her hand pulled free of Niko's, and the small shrine maiden somersaulted forward and collapsed, while Niko stretched out her right hand again in an instinctive motion.

But that hand didn't get very far.

Two jet-black panels sprang up from the shadow spreading out at her feet and clapped around Niko. Orange sparks shot off the entire body of the small avatar.

"Ah...Aaaaaah!!" Here, finally, a shout that was more like a scream gushed out of his throat.

Kuroyukihime and the others, getting ready to start the next meeting, whirled around and saw the situation in the distance.

The very first to react was Blood Leopard. She had no sooner howled in animalistic rage than she was leaping forward with all her might. She activated Beast Mode in midair, and when the crimson leopard touched down on the grass, she raced toward the Red King at a tremendous speed.

But the purple laser fired once more in the distance and plunged into the ground at Leopard's feet. The cat avatar was forced to leap from side to side to avoid the beams of light that came this time, one at a time, with a built-in delay. During that time, the jet-black panels pinning Niko steadily pushed closer together. The Red King appeared to be fighting back as hard as she could, but she couldn't win out against the pressure, perhaps due to her exhaustion.

"Run!" Kuroyukihime shouted, and they all kicked at the ground at the same time.

On his third step, Haruyuki jumped, spread his wings, and accelerated all at once. Forty meters until the imprisoned Niko... Thirty...

But then the gap between the two panels finally closed. There was no death effect. Niko was being held prisoner in the panels.

The matte-black rectangular solids, reflecting absolutely no light, began to sink once more into the shadow reaching across the surface of the earth.

"Black...Viiiiiiise!!" Flying at top speed, Haruyuki yelled the name of his hated enemy.

There was no mistake. Those black panels were the transformed figure of the self-proclaimed vice president of the Acceleration Research Society, Black Vise. And the one firing the purple laser was the Quad Eyes Analyst, Argon Array.

He wouldn't let them. He totally was not going to let them abduct Niko. Gritting his teeth so hard they almost shattered, Haruyuki flew.

On the building in the distance, the purple light flashed again. Haruyuki caught the attacking laser with the light-guiding rod of his left arm and reflected it. Then he brandished his right hand.

Twenty meters ahead of him, the rectangular body had sunk more than 70 percent into the shadow.

"Laser...Lance!!"

The long lance of silver light that shot forward dug deeply into the side of the black panel. But its descent didn't stop.

Plrp. Leaving a black ripple behind, the panel sank into the shadow at the exact moment Haruyuki was thrusting his right hand into that very spot. Propelled by all the momentum from his flight, his right hand pushed into the earth nearly to his elbow. However, his fingertips touched nothing.

"Graaar!!" Catching up with him, Leopard dug into the earth with her claws, roaring. But all that she found was virtual soil; the black panels did not come out.

Black Vise had the ability to move freely within shadows. Once he sank into them, finding him from outside was...

—No, there's still time!!

Haruyuki yanked his hand out of the earth and stood. He helped Utai up from where she landed, right next to the spot where Niko disappeared, and handed her to Fuko.

He wouldn't give up. He absolutely would not give up. He took a deep breath and tried to somehow take back control of his thoughts burning too hot with rage.

"Pard, please chase down Argon! Someone, leave through the nearest portal and pull Niko's cable!" Giving these instructions in a single breath, Haruyuki kicked at the ground again. He rapidly ascended to an altitude of thirty meters and scanned the surroundings.

The buildings of the Twilight stage were mostly pillar, so there were plenty of gaps and openings. The shadows that were Black Vise's special roadways had to be cut off somewhere. And Vise would be heading not toward the base of Midtown Tower, but the edge. Because the tower was an independent building, and the first floor wasn't in contact with the shadow of any other building.

Chasing the tower's shadow with his eyes, the leading edge jutted out of the park and fused with the shadow of a building somewhere around where Argon was. Vise would appear just once, somewhere up there. Haruyuki couldn't miss that moment.

He needed to open up his field of view—focus not on one point, but on the whole. The number of buildings was vast, and the paths of the shadows were linked in complicated ways, but he had to look at them all at the same time.

Leopard was running north in the park, chasing after Argon Array. Beyond that, in a narrow alleyway a little ways from the park, a purple reflection flashed. That was probably Argon. If Vise was joining up with her...Farther past that. Right around the place where a cluster of temples cut across...

Then Haruyuki saw it. From a shadow stretching out into the center of a large intersection, a jet-black rectangular body sliding upward.

Niko!!

I promised! I said I'll protect you! That I'd come flying if you were ever in a jam!!

He turned the emotions that exploded in the center of his avatar into energy. He gathered up every image of light in the wings on his back and shouted, "Light Speed!!" A silver overlay jetted from his wings, and his duel avatar flew furiously.

In the distant intersection, the black rectangular body transformed into a human silhouette and began to cross the road. His arms held a red avatar, which had apparently lost consciousness.

Beyond the intersection was the next shadow. If Vise escaped into that, Haruyuki wouldn't be able to follow him farther.

More. More. More speed.

A sense of hyper acceleration came over him, and the world changed color. The stretched-out time became a viscous wall, blocking the way forward.

More. More...

If you wish for it so badly...

Once more, that voice—he thought it had gone off somewhere, but again, he heard the voice of Archangel Metatron.

I shall lend you my power this once. Now call it out loud. My name.

In the top left of his field of view, a row of text in the system color flashed: You got an Enhanced Armament: Metatron Wings.

In his accelerated consciousness, Haruyuki shouted, "Equip! Metatron Wiiiiiiings!!"

A pure-white light poured down from the heavens and hit his back. Another pair of wings formed above the metallic ones that were already there. Whiter than anything, thin like blades, but concealing a fearsome power: angel wings.

A dizzying propulsive force slammed into the entire body of Silver Crow, already accelerating with Incarnate. The tips of the fingers of his outstretched hands pierced the wall of time standing in his way.

"F...lyyyyyyyyyyyyyyyy!!"

Four wings shining, Haruyuki became a beam of light and flew.

To be continued.

AFTERWORD

Thank you for reading *Accel World 14: Archangel of Savage Light*.

I, Kawahara, promised in the afterword of the previous book, Volume 13, that I'd be able to finish the Metatron attack arc in four volumes, that I definitely wouldn't make it five. Those of you who have already finished reading the book by the time you read this afterword are aware that, while there is indeed an attack on the Legend-class Enemy Archangel Metatron, just two pages before the words you are reading now came the dreaded "To be continued"…

Whether or not, in the end, it can be said that the Metatron attack arc is complete, I would like to leave that decision to future historians— No, I'm sorry. It isn't finished, is it? No matter how you look at it. This double-header with Seiryu and Metatron was not just an intense mission for Haruyuki and the others but for me as well…V-volume 15 will definitely…probably…

Now, then. All of that is to say that this was the first all-avatar edition in the history of *AW* (although strictly speaking, they did burst out for just a moment halfway through). The first part was at 12:20 PM real-world time, while in the last pages, it was probably around 12:20:57 PM, so this single book doesn't even take a whole minute in the real world. Even I myself do wonder a little about this, but it might be a record for shortest time among all the Dengeki novels! It makes me a little happy to think about that— No, I'm sorry. I've learned my lesson. I'll work hard to deliver the next volume as soon as I can, so I do hope you'll join me just a little longer for the Metatron attack arc, now the ISS kit arc!

Changing the subject, I was invited to Sakura-Con, an anime convention held in Seattle, Washington, in the United States, so I crossed the Pacific Ocean for the first time in my life from the end of March to the beginning of April. I have far too many impressions to write them all down here in this limited space, but I was happily surprised at the fact that on the other side of the ocean, an incredible number of people in the US passionately love Japanese anime and manga. Unfortunately, the majority of light novels are not translated and published (including *Accel* and *SAO*), but I really do think how nice it would be if they were able to someday enjoy the original novels. I'd like to take this opportunity to extend my deepest gratitude to the organizers of Sakura-Con; everyone from Aniplex of America, who kindly attended; and Hirai from the Dengeki Editorial Division, who came with me from Japan.

To conclude, then, I sincerely apologize to illustrator HIMA and to my editor Miki, both of whom I inconvenienced at a more malicious level than ever in *Accel* history with the difficult journey due to the many, many characters appearing in this volume (a party of nine is simply too large...). And to all of you who have been kind enough to come along with me this far, the greatest gratitude in the history of *Accel*! Next time for sure, I will end it!

Reki Kawahara
On a certain day in April 2013

ACCEL WORLD, Volume 14
REKI KAWAHARA

Translation by Jocelyne Allen
Cover art by HIMA

ACCEL WORLD Vol. 14
© REKI KAWAHARA 2013
First published in Japan in 2013 by KADOKAWA CORPORATION,
Tokyo.
English translation rights arranged with KADOKAWA CORPORA-
TION, Tokyo, through Tuttle-Mori Agency, Inc., Tokyo.

English translation © 2018 by Yen Press, LLC

Yen On
1290 Avenue of the Americas
New York, NY 10104

Visit us at yenpress.com
facebook.com/yenpress
twitter.com/yenpress
yenpress.tumblr.com
instagram.com/yenpress

First Yen On Edition: June 2018

Yen On is an imprint of Yen Press, LLC.
The Yen On name and logo are trademarks of Yen Press, LLC.

Library of Congress Cataloging-in-Publication Data
Names: Kawahara, Reki, author. I HIMA (Comic book artist) illustrator. I
    Beepee, designer. I Allen, Jocelyne, 1974– translator.
Title: Accel World / Reki Kawahara ; illustrations, HIMA ; design, bee-pee ;
    translation by Jocelyne Allen.
Description: First Yen On edition. I New York, NY : Yen On, 2014–
Identifiers: LCCN 2014025099 I ISBN 9780316376730 (v. 1 : pbk.) I
    ISBN 9780316296366 (v. 2 : pbk.) I ISBN 9780316296373 (v. 3 : pbk.) I
    ISBN 9780316296380 (v. 4 : pbk.) I ISBN 9780316296397 (v. 5 : pbk.) I
    ISBN 9780316296403 (v. 6 : pbk.) I ISBN 9780316358194 (v. 7 : pbk.) I
    ISBN 9780316317610 (v. 8 : pbk.) I ISBN 9780316502702 (v. 9 : pbk.) I
    ISBN 9780316466059 (v. 10 : pbk.) I ISBN 9780316466066 (v. 11 : pbk.) I
    ISBN 9780316466073 (v. 12 : pbk.) I ISBN 9781975300067 (v. 13 : pbk.) I
    ISBN 9781975327231 (v. 14 : pbk.)
Subjects: I CYAC: Science fiction. I Virtual reality—Fiction. I Fantasy.
Classification: LCC PZ7.K1755Kaw 2014 I DDC [Fic]—dc23
LC record available at https://lccn.loc.gov/2014025099

ISBNs: 978-1-9753-2723-1 (paperback)
       978-1-9753-2724-8 (ebook)

10 9 8 7 6 5 4 3 2 1

LSC-C

Printed in the United States of America